ADAPTATIONS

JILL THRUSSELL

ISBN: 0993389902
ISBN-13: 978-0993389900

CONTENTS

JILTED LOVERS

Genesis prepared to leave the daily duty of work behind him as excitement bubbled inside his veins, he was meeting Cherise, his girlfriend whom he'd been involved in a highly, passionate, exciting relationship with for approximately five months now, at the plush restaurant and wine bar they usually frequented on special occasions. The venue situated in the heart of the city was luxurious and the expenditure Genesis knew was extravagant but today's occasion warranted the additional expense. Genesis slipped a small ring box out of his trouser pocket and opened it as the diamond inside implanted into a bed of platinum shone, glistened and sparkled as particles of light bounced off it, today was the day he would propose to the woman who had captured his heart and captivated him, from the very first moment they'd met. He'd planned everything precisely, he'd engage her for a year and save up for a lavish wedding, he'd spare no expense, then perhaps they'd move out of the city and settle down somewhere then they'd have some beautiful children together.

The city street buzzed with noise as he walked briskly out of the glass doors that led into the offices where he worked, a man on a dedicated mission that quite simply had to be fulfilled that very same day. It was now or never, he'd finally plucked up the courage to propose and there was to be absolutely no backing down now. He took a deep breath as he walked towards his destiny and contemplated his proposal. Deep down Genesis knew his means were far from satisfactory when it came to the lavish lifestyle Cherise could possibly have. His job wasn't much to talk about, he was a simple computer technician for a sales company but it was honest work and it paid the bills. He rushed down the street filled with eager shoppers as he avoided the bodies of strangers as they passed him, their arms laden with bags full of purchases and glanced down at his phone to quickly check the time, it was getting late. He was very much aware now, he didn't have long to reach to the restaurant he'd selected as the location for what might be the most important appointment of his entire adult life.

A shopper suddenly bumped into him as he walked as they appeared as if from nowhere. Neither party had been paying full attention to the sidewalk, distracted by the excitement and wonder of the evenings activities and their various agendas and the collision had been resulted in a hard, sharp knock to them both. Genesis smiled and apologized humbly as he turned to face the attractive looking female, he'd just collided with.

"I'm so sorry." Genesis insisted as he picked up a bag she'd dropped as a result of their collision and handed it back to her politely.

"No really it's my fault. I wasn't looking where I was going." The woman replied as she opened the bag and gazed into it in order to inspect the goods she'd just purchased for possible breakages. "I hope it's not broken, it's a toy for my daughter, she's wanted one for a while. It's her birthday this weekend." She remarked as she pulled a small, robotic dog out of the bag that had been situated inside a cardboard box. She gazed down at it in dismay as she realized the robotic dog's head now dangled down in a sultry silence, it was definitely broken and Samaria knew her daughter Charlotte would be absolutely heartbroken.

A look of deep sadness crossed Samaria's face as Genesis smiled and quickly attempted to reassure her. He quickly plucked his wallet out from the back pocket of his trousers and handed her a wad of notes.

"I hope that covers it." He insisted.

"Are you sure? Really I couldn't. I mean it was as much my fault as yours." Samaria said politely.

Genesis nodded eagerly in response. "I insist."

"Well I guess if you're really sure. It is Charlotte's birthday after all and they do cost an arm and a leg. She'd be heartbroken if she didn't receive a gift, she's wanted one of these for a while."

"I'm very sure and buy her a little something from me too." Genesis replied as he handed her another couple of notes from his open wallet.

"Thank you so much. I'm Samaria." Samaria remarked as she observed that Genesis had actually handed to her, two hundred dollars in total. She smiled appreciatively at his generosity.

"Nice to meet you. I'm Genesis." Genesis replied as he shook her hand gently. He glanced back down at his phone a few seconds later and quickly realized that the collision and conversation had delayed him slightly and that time was rapidly slipping away from his grasp as each second turned to minutes and the minutes quickly disappeared. He thought of a polite way to leave as he rushed to depart. "Sorry you'll have to excuse me. I really have to go. I have an appointment. I hope your daughter has a great birthday."

Samaria smiled and nodded appreciatively.

The two strangers bound only by an accidental collision, parted as Genesis walked briskly down the street towards his destination once more and Samaria headed back towards the shop that she'd just come out five minutes before. Samaria began to quietly contemplate further as she walked as to why she only met handsome, attractive men very briefly and why they never actually seemed to stay around very long. Within a few minutes, Genesis had entered her life and then simply departed from it and the moment of what could have been an exciting encounter and possible interlude to romance, had simply slipped through her fingers like drops of water and there was quite simply nothing at all she could do to stop each drop's disappearance. Genesis disappeared into the distance as Samaria accepted the fact, she'd let the moment and allowed a very eligible man, to slip straight out of her grasp. Genesis was gone and the brief introduction and possible opportunity for romance she'd been presented with had been regretfully lost.

A few minutes later, once Samaria arrived back inside the department store, she quickly scurried through the aisles as she shook her head and focused once more on the task at hand. She had to purchase another robotic dog and right now that was a lot more important than a missed meeting with what could have been Mr. Right. Dating often presented more problems and headache than it was worth, she mused, Genesis might be a really horrible person and perhaps his lack of availability was actually a blessing in disguise.

Genesis continued on his journey as he began to count the cost of the evening so far which had already escalated somewhat. The hidden costs he'd had to indulge in to make the evening perfect, had grown and he shook his head as he walked and thought about how much he'd already expended as he sighed, he hadn't even actually arrived at the restaurant yet. The engagement ring had cost him just over ten thousand dollars, the table reservation at the restaurant he'd selected a thousand dollars and now he'd spent another two hundred dollars in repairs and his night still hadn't even begun.

"Cherise better say yes." He muttered to himself quietly as he entered into the street where the restaurant was situated and headed towards it.

The restaurant entrance stood out from the other shops and venues that surrounded it as it shone and shimmered. It seemed to welcome him politely as particles of light bounced of the golden archway that led to the interior from the street lights nearby and droplets of water cascaded down either side of the archway as they glistened eagerly. The water gently bubbled down the pieces of glass situated at either side of the entrance and then slipped through two small, golden drains on the ground below as they disappeared, Genesis paused as he stood outside the venue for a moment and took a deep breath and then prepared to step into inside. His body trembled a little nervously.

Once inside the restaurant Genesis glanced around quickly and observed that the venue wasn't very busy yet as the evening rush hadn't actually started. He quickly sought out Cherise's presence and sighed with relief as he realized, she hadn't yet actually arrived. They were both running late and luckily for him, Cherise was running even later than he was, which on this occasion was actually a good thing as it gave him a chance to absorb his surroundings and prepare for her arrival. A waiter nearby approached him as he stood quietly inside the foyer.

"Do you have a reservation sir?" He asked politely.

"Yes it's under the name Genesis Galaway, but my date hasn't arrived yet, so I'd like to have a drink at the bar first." Genesis explained politely.

"No problem. Let me know when she arrives and I'll seat you both at your table." The waiter replied as he nodded.

The two men smiled at each other and then Genesis made his way over to the nearby bar to order a stiff drink. The bar itself was lined with high, cream and gold, colored leather stools that stood in a regimented line next to it, almost like soldiers guarding a precious object. The brightly lit mirrored backdrop had a golden tint to it, which matched the golden counter it was situated above and the entire restaurant looked elegant and expensive. Not only did it compliment the proposal he was preparing to make but also Cherise, who he knew appreciated the finer things in life. Tonight, he intended to give Cherise the best he possibly could, even if that was not always going to be possible, due to his moderate income. A few seconds later the waiter quickly scurried off to attend to tables situated in alcoves nearby that lined the exterior walls of the venue as he left Genesis alone seated beside the bar.

"Can I have a whisky on the rocks please." Genesis asked as a female server approached him. He sat down on one of the cream and gold bar stools by the bar and smiled politely at her as he placed his order.

"Certainly." She replied as she smiled in response.

An empty glass was taken out from below the bar counter and filled with the amber liquid Genesis had requested as she prepared his drink. Genesis glanced at the shiny, gold dress she wore for a moment as he watched her, it matched the interior décor that surrounded them and made the whole restaurant seem very color coordinated. The waiters and waitresses scattered around the restaurant were all dressed in similar colors, their bodies adorned with cream and gold outfits that shimmered as they walked and it denoted complete perfectionism. The proprietor had obviously put a lot of thought into not only the décor but also the employees attire, which matched the venue with artistic precision. The drink Genesis had requested, arrived within a few seconds and he knocked it back extremely quickly, relieved as if somehow the amber, brown liquid would provide him with the last ounce of courage he needed to pose the question he'd held in his heart since the moment he'd met the woman he actually wanted to betroth.

After approximately five minutes of waiting, Genesis gasped with excitement as he glanced over towards the entrance of the restaurant and Cherise entered inside. Her mere arrival excited him. Cherise wore a long white and gold shimmering dress, that shone as particles of light bounced of it as she walked. Parts of her naked flesh were exposed as he glanced at her flat, toned stomach, through the cut out pieces of material that created oval holes, situated at both sides of her waist. She looked as sophisticated and elegant as usual. Her sensual, cherry, full red lips and black, flowing ringlets, adorned her face and neck almost like jewelry that had been placed there precisely. The creator had definitely put everything in exactly the right place, when it came to Cherise's physical architecture, Genesis thought. Cherise looked absolutely fantastic.

Once inside the venue, Cherise paused by the entrance for a few seconds as she glanced quickly around the large room and searched for Genesis. A few seconds later Cherise smiled as she noticed him and nodded her head to acknowledge his presence, she then quickly made her way towards him.

The breath-taking moment of Cherise's arrival which had excited Genesis, caused him to fidget as he rubbed his hands together happily and eagerly anticipated what the evening ahead might bring. Excitement continued to bubble away inside him just under the surface of his skin, like a pot of soup that simmered away gently on top of a hot stove as she drew closer. This was their moment he thought, the moment he would commit his life to her, the moment he'd waited for anxiously for the past two months ever since he'd made the decision. Two months ago, he'd actually decided that the time was right and that he was going to be brave enough to take the plunge and ask Cherise to engage him. Although he'd actually known he wanted to marry Cherise from the first moment they'd met, he'd often lacked the courage to approach the topic and discuss it with her and many times the words he longed to say, had simply sat behind his lips unasked and obstructed by fear. Two months ago however, Genesis had finally pushed himself to actually organize his proposal and now the moment of realization had finally arrived.

"Hi Genesis." Cherise remarked quite casually, seemingly oblivious to the underlying reason for the occasion as she kissed him gently on the cheek to greet him.

The casualness Cherise displayed towards him, didn't put Genesis off as he eagerly slid of the bar stool he'd been seated on and drew closer to her as he kissed her on the cheek in response. "I've made reservations." Genesis replied enthusiastically as he held Cherise's arm gently and began to lead her away from the bar towards a table situated inside an alcove nearby. "The tables ready. I booked our usual table."

There was an awkward moment of silence between them as Cherise shook her head and Genesis observed a slight hesitation on her part as she resisted him and stood rooted firmly to the spot. Sadness seemed to fill her eyes as Genesis searched his mind and wondered what could possibly be going on inside her brain for a moment. Confusion flooded through his body as fear threw his thoughts and emotions into an instant whirlpool of upset. Genesis suddenly began to feel slightly unsteady as the turmoil inside him grew and started to consume him.

For the past two months, Genesis had embarked on a journey of exploration as he'd walked out across the deep abyss of the marriage proposal he intended to make. He'd balanced himself delicately on the small, thin pole that hung over its depths and ventured into the area of a real lifelong commitment, something he'd quite simply never, ever actually done before. The marriage proposal once made he knew couldn't be retracted and Genesis had taken each step across the narrow pole, towards the other side and crossed the pit of possible rejection, very carefully. He'd waited patiently for his moment and he'd gauged Cherise's commitment to him as he'd prepared. If Cherise simply said no right now he knew deep down inside that he would immediately topple off the very thin pole and rapidly fall down into the depths of her rejection. That fall it was highly unlikely Genesis would actually be unable to salvage himself or his heart from and the bombshell of despair such rejection created afterwards would be difficult to cope with.

ADAPTATIONS

"Sit down for a moment please Genesis. There's something I have to tell you." Cherise insisted softly as she gently led him back towards the bar stool once more.

Confusion continued to spiral and somersault through Genesis's thoughts as it rushed through his mind like a speeding train, his eyes became clouded and seemed to blur for a few seconds. Obediently however a minute later, he stepped back towards the bar and sat down on the bar stool once more with a somewhat glum expression on his face as he waited for Cherise to break his heart. For a split second, Genesis felt almost like a naughty school boy, who'd not done his homework that was being scolded by a teacher. He could tell from the tone of Cherise's voice that this was not going to be a pretty conversation and that whatever she said next would definitely upset him. Before Cherise even opened her mouth to speak the words that lay within her heart and mind that yearned to escape from her lips, Genesis could sense the news she had to tell him was going to be absolutely devastating and he would definitely not like it.

"It's no good Genesis." Cherise explained sadly. "There's something I need to say and it's not good news I'm afraid." She explained as she gazed into his eyes pitifully and shook her head. "I've given this relationship everything I can and things are just not really working out for me." She continued in a much quieter tone almost as if she actually felt guilty about every word she spoke.

A moment of silence wrapped itself around them both as it sat firmly in-between them as it became almost deafening. Genesis's body started to become numb with shock. The occupants inside the restaurant that surrounded them, seemed to evaporate quickly as the strangers faded into the background and disappeared. Somehow they seemed to merge into the furniture situated nearby as Genesis found himself alone with Cherise. The tone of her voice and the words she spoke said absolutely everything he needed to know but deep down inside Genesis simply couldn't accept defeat, not now, not here and certainly not today. He quickly reached within himself and managed to pull out a final plea as he attempted to salvage the proposal he intended to make and his dedication to Cherise, both of which he yearned for her to accept. He couldn't simply sit back and let her walk away, walk away from him, his marriage proposal and his world.

The silence between them prompted Genesis to reflect for a moment on the very first moment they'd met as images of his initial meeting with Cherise had filled his mind. He'd attended a salsa class with a work colleague as they'd roped him to enjoying a night out and enticed him to attend, the possibility of meeting attractive females that were looking for love, fun and some intertwining dance movements had been a convincing argument presented to him and Genesis had agreed to participate. He'd succumbed and participated in his colleague's request, even though music, dancing and salsa wasn't particularly his kind of thing. Cherise had appeared throughout the evening almost like a Goddess and had playfully pulled him to his feet and onto the dance floor to dance with her once the salsa class he'd actually attended had finished and the wine bar had transformed into a club environment. His work colleague who had by this time deserted him, had simply left him sitting at a table with a drink as he'd disappeared and headed off to the club dance floor with a partner he'd found to dance with.

The offer to dance with Cherise had been like a Godsend to Genesis who seemed to have two left feet which meant he wasn't particularly competent or fluid in his movements. His inabilities hadn't seemed to bother Cherise however, who'd simply laughed them off as he'd explained them to her.

"We weren't born dancing Genesis. It's something you have to learn." Cherise had teased as she led him onto the floor and smiled. "I'll show you some moves."

The two had danced into the early hours of the morning and Genesis had been reluctant to depart from her arms, her touch and her smile as the event had drawn to a close and the music stopped playing. They'd exchanged numbers and Genesis had called her every single day ever since. Their venture into the area of romance had been a very natural progression as they'd become closer and Genesis quite simply couldn't believe his luck. An innocent night out to participate in a fun, odd activity had actually transcended into the most special relationship of his life and he was grateful that it had and that he had actually attended. The salsa club disappeared as the picture within his mind faded and he paid attention once more to his current situation and the important conversation he was currently engaged in. A conversation that would ultimately determine his path for the rest of his life.

"Please Cherise you can't do this." Genesis gasped desperately as he clutched for straws of hope in her eyes and some kind of reassurance that her remark had simply been a prank. "Not now. I'll try harder, I'll make it work. I can be better, I'll do whatever you want me to. I can make you happy." He pleaded as her negative words began to sink into his mind and the serious, sad expression on her face hit him like a brick of reality.

Cherise was deadly serious as a more solemn expression crossed her face and no reassurances were forthcoming. "Genesis, there's actually something I haven't told you." She explained a little sheepishly as she continued. "Something you definitely won't like."

There was a pause for a few seconds as Genesis stared into at her eyes wounded and hurt; his eyes were filled with pain as he accepted that the ugly conversation he was involved in was actually about to become even uglier. He struggled to catch his breath as his body sank onto the bar stool that he was perched on top off. His body seemed to collapse as his shoulders slumped down onto the top of his spine in a heap. Genesis was hurt, broken and humiliated as his body crumbled and he struggled to carry the heaviness of his own weight.

"There's someone else Genesis. I've been seeing them for a while. I'm going away to another country." Cherise explained. "We're going away, together."

The words cut through Genesis's heart like a knife as he bore the pain of the stab of her attack and her betrayal. He attempted to swallow as his pride stuck in his throat like a lump, but his throat grated like sandpaper, dry and parched. He took a deep breath and asserted himself as he decided he would actually try to make one last attempt to save his relationship. He'd spent a lot of money, he waited for two months and he was determined at the very least he wasn't going to make this easy for Cherise. She simply couldn't just walk away from him, not now, not today. Genesis took a deep breath as he attempted to muster his strength and prepared to plead with

Cherise one final time. He decided as he reflected upon the unfaithfulness Cherise had confessed to, that he would actually forgive her, he'd love her and he'd accept her wrongs. The ugly betrayal of the past would be forgotten and they'd walk into a more committed, beautiful future and he'd shed the remnants of hurt, that this conversation had actually created. He simply couldn't face losing Cherise, not now, not like this.

"I wanted to propose to you today." Genesis explained softly. "I still can."

The suggestion Genesis made was immediately rejected as soon as it arrived and entered into Cherise's ears as she shook her head immediately in response. She touched his hand softly as Genesis's heart sank to the bottom of his feet as if it was a rock sinking to the bottom of a deep, dark lake as waves of hopelessness washed over him. She'd thrown a stone of rejection at him, that had plunged rapidly into the depths of his soul and the couple's relationship was becoming more and more unsalvageable with every word she uttered.

"It's no good Genesis. I can't give you what you seek." Cherise insisted quietly. "We'd be living a lie, you would be chaining a heart bound by duty that would never truly be yours." Cherise paused for a moment as she glanced into his eyes sadly. She could see Genesis's head now hung down low as if somehow burdened by the heaviness of her words. "Forgive me and forget me Genesis and as your heart heals, I promise you, one day, you will smile again." She urged softly as she attempted to reassure him. "I don't deserve you Genesis, believe me."

The final words Cherise spoke touched Genesis for a few seconds and he felt slightly comforted for a moment, but a few seconds later that comfort was quickly interrupted by another thought as he speculated that perhaps Cherise had just said those words to comfort him and that really, the words actually meant nothing to her at all, like how now he actually meant nothing to her at all. Someone else had broken into their relationship and stolen her heart like a thief by stealth and he hadn't even noticed it, they had taken his place and become significant to her as they'd seized the place in her heart, he had once occupied. Someone had stolen the heart that he had worshipped and that had previously, been dedicated only to him. Perhaps, he thought, she'd even rehearsed this whole speech before she'd actually arrived as he glanced up at Cherise's face once more, weary and totally defeated.

Each second seemed to last an eternity as they struggled with their internal desires, Genesis's desire to retain the relationship and Cherise's desire to depart from it. A few seconds later however, Cherise simply ended the discussion and the relationship as she leant forward towards him, kissed him on the forehead and then simply walked away silently. Genesis watched her depart as his head spun around and around with confusion as he deliberated for a moment whether or not he should actually attempt to pursue her. Perhaps, he thought, he could plead with her one more time, beg her, convince her to stay and perhaps she would realize in that split second, how much he loved her and that no one else could possibly love her that way. Perhaps she would see how much he deserved her love, how faithful he'd actually been and how devoted to her, he really was.

A few seconds later as Cherise disappeared from sight Genesis shook his head gently as he accepted the reality, she was already gone and pleading with her now, would simply reinforce, how pathetic and dependent on her, he actually was for his happiness. Deep down inside now he knew no matter what he said to her, it would change nothing and that he would simply end looking even more useless in her sight. Genesis accepted the void that her rejection had created within him as he realized that within a few minutes, Cherise had actually buried their relationship and that now, only the companionship of rejection remained.

The waiter approached him a few minutes later and coughed as he cleared his throat and attempted to attract Genesis's attention to his presence. "Are you ready for your table now Sir?" He asked politely.

"I won't be needing the reservation anymore." Genesis explained as he glanced into his eyes sadly. He quickly stood up, opened up his wallet and handed the waiter a thousand dollars. "Apologies for the cancellation."

The waiter nodded in understanding as he accepted the money graciously and then disappeared abruptly. The waiter, Genesis thought could probably sense that he'd just been dumped and he didn't blame him for his rapid disappearance, such situations were tricky and finding the right words to comfort a stranger in those circumstances could be difficult.

The restaurant seemed to fade into the background once more as Genesis walked slowly towards the exit, there would be no meal tonight, no joyous celebration of unity, now there were only shadows of rejection, despair and division that clung to the particles of air as he walked through them, that seemed to mock his heartbreak. The tables around him were filled with couples and their laughter and joy seemed to taunt his broken heart as he passed by each one quietly. Once he arrived at the restaurant door, he simply pushed his way through it as he stumbled out onto the street nearby and gasped for fresh air. A numbness inside him overwhelmed him as it started to fill every ounce of his body. He walked back down the street outside the restaurant quietly that he'd entered just an hour earlier, his heart filled with hope, joy and eager expectations, now however he was a shadow of his former self and filled with only despair, sadness, hurt and pain.

The street itself was much quieter and emptier as the shops situated around the restaurant had all closed and the bustling shoppers had disappeared. That was one relief, Genesis thought there were now less people around to face in his broken state. Genesis quickly found a quiet bar in a nearby side street and entered inside as he decided to drown his sorrows with some alcoholic medication. Country music played in the background as it wafted through the air and into his ears as he stepped inside the bar. The volume of the music was relatively low and inside the bar, there were just a few customers scattered around the interior, seated at the tables alone or in small groups. Genesis passed them quietly as he approached the bar. The lighting inside the bar was dim which coupled with the music, presented a mellow, soothing ambience and that provided a slight comfort him as he walked.

The Landlord a man in his early fifties quickly attended to Genesis as he sat down on a bar stool nearby. He rushed over towards him, glanced at his face and then plucked out an empty glass from underneath the bar. Both men seemed to instantly understand each other as the Landlord quickly poured some whisky into the glass and nodded at him in a reassuring manner. The drink was accepted and appreciated as Genesis knocked the contents of the glass back quickly and a few seconds later placed the empty glass back down on the bar. He nodded at the Landlord as he ordered a refill silently and the empty glass was quickly refilled. Genesis quickly drank the contents of the glass once more.

"Better yet?" The Landlord asked.

Genesis shook his head. "Not quite yet. A couple more perhaps."

The landlord obliged obediently and filled the glass once more as the two men faced each other at opposite sides of the bar in silence. Genesis placed the ring box on top of the bar and handed the Landlord some money from his wallet courteously. Filled with the sorrows that engulfed his spirit, Genesis quickly tried to drown his heartbreak as he continued to consume the brown liquid that he'd just been served.

A few hours passed by before the Landlord started to prepare to close the bar for the night and Genesis stumbled back out onto the street and hailed a cab. He'd left his car parked outside work earlier that evening and had decided to collect it the next day as he'd had absolutely no intention of driving home that night. The plan Genesis had made, meant that he'd actually intended to enjoy the champagne the restaurant offered with Cherise as they'd celebrated their engagement and even though his evening had actually deviated from that plan, deep down inside he knew, he was in no fit state to drive himself home or anywhere else that night.

Regardless of how much pain Cherise had inflicted on him and no matter how upset he was, Genesis knew that night, he still had to go home, sleep and then actually attend work the next day. Reality was not kind and Mr. Ferdinand, Genesis's boss would care little about the wounds that had been inflicted onto his heart the previous night and Genesis knew it. His boss wasn't the romantic type and he cared little for personal matters when it came to work attendance, absences and lateness. In Mr. Ferdinand's world and business, lateness and absences due to personal issues, were simply occurrences that were just totally unacceptable to him and he had absolutely no compassion regarding broken hearts at all. If Genesis actually failed to attend work the next day, he would indeed be disciplined and it really was that simple. There was no possibility of calling in and pretending to be sick, due to a hangover and broken heart, such excuses were simply out of the question if Genesis actually wanted to remain employed. Mr. Ferdinand, ran a very tight ship and he could see through weak, pretentious excuses very easily. His only concern seemed to be that Genesis and the rest of his team, arrived on time, left on time and were productive as possible whilst in attendance. Genesis's boss was strict and he'd always made it very clear to everyone who worked for him, his business was not a playground.

Unfortunately when the next morning arrived predictably, Genesis was late for work, his body suffering from the effects of his alcoholic indulgence the night before as he clocked in at the reception desk glumly and glanced at the time on the huge white and black clock that hung on the wall above the reception desk. Although he'd actually rushed to work, it had been impossible to avoid the inevitable sluggishness in his system due to his activities the prior night and he'd arrived thirty minutes later than he was supposed to. He'd glanced at the large grey building as he'd approached it and groaned, he'd exceeded his bosses five minute tolerance threshold for lateness and he'd immediately known, there would be no escaping the scrutiny he'd face as a result.

He avoided exchanging smiles and pleasantries with the receptionist a mature, pleasant woman that greeted everyone with a smile everyday as he'd rushed towards the elevator nearby, he was late enough already. Once inside the elevator Genesis reached inside his trouser pocket and quickly found two painkillers that he washed down with a mouthful of the black coffee, he'd actually managed to purchase on his way to work. The building itself today for some reason seemed unusually quiet Genesis thought as he made his way towards his desk quietly, anxious not to draw any more attention to his lateness than was actually necessary. He walked past some workstations occupied by some of his colleagues as they worked away quietly, unusually however, they didn't even glance up at him to acknowledge him as he passed them. Something was very wrong and Genesis could feel it. The look on each of their faces as he glanced at them seemed to be one of devastation as they stared directly in front of them and focused on their tasks intensely as if they were picking up the pieces of debris that some kind of destruction had left behind, that he had not yet been exposed to. It was almost as if a storm had passed through the office block, ravaged the building and destroyed the usual comradery that he was accustomed to. Genesis could sense that something was indeed very wrong, but what exactly that was, had not become evident to him yet.

A few seconds later as Genesis sat down in front of his workstation in the partition of the office that housed him each day, he quickly touched the screen in front of him as he turned on his system. He had no desire to actually delay his work duties for a second longer than was possible and his screen lit up instantly as he sat down in front of it. Genesis immediately checked his email inbox as he usually did each morning, before he actually started to attend to his other routine tasks and found an unopened email waiting for him, it was from human resources.

Perhaps, Genesis thought for a second Cherise was right, what could he possibly give her, she was a beautiful, jet setting model and he was a simple, working class man that struggled to provide a lifestyle for her, that he could not actually afford to accommodate. He wasn't overly handsome whilst she was stunningly beautiful and he definitely wasn't wealthy enough to provide her with the lifestyle he knew, she was used to. Perhaps he thought, he'd actually been fooling himself when he'd believed that one day Cherise would actually marry him. Her confession had perhaps simply been an honest admission of events that they both knew, one day, would eventually happen, no matter what he had or hadn't done. Perhaps Cherise had simply spared him from the devastating impact that a future divorce could bring and the complications of the heart broken children they might have given life to if they'd actually married. Perhaps Cherise had been cruel to him in the short term, to actually avoid being crueler to him in the longer term.

ADAPTATIONS

The email in front of him distracted Genesis from his thoughts as it demanded his attention and he opened it, the subject simply read 'Urgent' as Genesis attempted to focus on the contents and pushed thoughts of Cherise for a moment, towards the back of his mind.

'Due to a significant restructuring, we are regrettably having to make thirty posts redundant. You are receiving this email as your post has been identified as one that will no longer be required.'

The contents of the email shocked Genesis as he absorbed and digested the words that appeared on the screen in front of him with disbelief and horror.

'Your redundancy payment along with a ten thousand dollar gratuity payment for your five years of service will be paid into your account on Friday. You are immediately released from service and you are required to hand in your security pass at reception by lunch time today.'

The email stunned Genesis as he read it over and over again totally confused. Five years of loyal service he'd given to this company and now he was simply being dismissed by an email almost as if his existence and contributions were totally irrelevant. He opened one of the drawers of the light beige desk he was seated in front of and found an empty box inside it. He knew immediately what it represented as he took the box out and started to fill it with his belongings that lay strewn across the top of his desk. He picked up his personal items and dropped each one into the box as he glanced solemnly at the photo of Cherise he always kept on the top of his desk. Genesis shook his head as he picked it up along with the photo of his parents and dropped them both inside the box. The photo of his parents made him smile for a split second as it reminded him of the times they'd spent together when he was a child. They'd prepared Genesis for life sufficiently he concluded, he was a hardworking, loyal, committed man but they hadn't prepared him for the seeds of rejection that now lay scattered around his heart as they rooted themselves deep into his veins and spread throughout his body like a plague.

Branches of despair gripped his throat and Genesis almost choked as each one tightened until they became almost suffocating. In the past twenty four hours his whole life had been totally destroyed, everything he knew, everything he cherished and everything he lived for, had been taken away from him in one foul swoop. There were no apologies and there was nothing comforting to replace what he'd lost. There was no job waiting for him, no other woman he could call to appease his loneliness, just a huge, empty void of nothing, that wrapped its arms around him and attempted to consume him as he wrestled with the crippling rejections that pelted him from every direction and every area of his life.

The box seemed to fill up quite quickly as Genesis continued to pack away his personal belongings silently. Once he'd finished, he simply picked up the box and walked towards the elevator quietly. He avoided eye contact with any of his colleagues as he walked past their partitions, his eyes cast firmly down towards the ground. They seemed very much absorbed in their own tasks and oblivious to his broken state as he passed them and absolutely none of them interrupted his departure. He speculated further for a moment as he walked as to why he'd been chosen and why his work colleagues that remained seated at their desks, hadn't.

Perhaps he concluded as he walked, when he'd applied for the promotion six months ago and it hadn't been given to him, his application had indicated that he was dissatisfied with his current job. Perhaps Mr. Ferdinand had assumed it would just be a matter of time before he'd seek another position elsewhere and leave anyway. The dismissal was perhaps preemptive of what they actually expected from him in the near future. Answers to his questions were not forthcoming however, no answers had actually been provided to him and now he knew, it was unlikely that they ever actually would be.

Once he reached the reception on the ground floor, Genesis simply handed in his security pass to the receptionist who was seated behind the grey, matt desk as instructed and prepared to leave. The receptionist glanced up at him and smiled sympathetically as he stood in front of her for a moment, the box that contained his belongings sat in his arms as she shook her head gently.

"Take care of yourself Genesis." The receptionist remarked politely as she nodded at him.

ADAPTATIONS

It was almost as if she'd been instructed to actually be polite to him Genesis thought, her words sounded mechanical and empty, void of any empathy or care. Genesis forced himself to smile at her for a second before he departed from her presence. The receptionist, a mature woman in her fifties had always greeted him with a smile each morning and there was no reason to actually be rude or dismissive towards her, after all his departure wasn't her decision and she had absolutely no control over the decision that had made at all. She'd no longer smile at him each morning, Genesis thought as he walked briskly away, pushed open the exterior glass doors of the building and stepped back outside into the cold street. He simply couldn't offer her a more positive response at that moment in time and Genesis was scared that if he actually even attempted to do so, he might break down completely.

The whole world had slipped away from Genesis almost as if an earthquake had attacked his life and all the pieces he'd once treasured and built through hard work, dedication and love, had simply sunk through the cracks it had left behind in the ground. Genesis had lost his whole world in a day and there was no sign of a forthcoming rescue or any kind redemption and that reality was quite simply, soul destroying. His heart was crushed and had been torn apart almost as if someone had broken into his body, ripped it out of his ribcage, torn it up and then simply thrown it onto the ground, to be trampled on by anyone who passed by. The devastation sank into his heart as Genesis accepted the negative events of the past twenty four hours and fully absorbed them in his mind, it had been as if a herd of buffalo had stampeded over his body as they'd crushed his entire spirit without warning. Now Genesis understood the harshness life could deliver, now Genesis understood rejection and now as he grieved the death of his relationship and career at the company he'd served faithfully for years, now Genesis finally understood loss.

OPPORTUNITIES

The next morning, Genesis awoke with a migraine as it pounded away like a hammer inside his head until it ached as he groaned. He rubbed his forehead and then quickly reached out towards his beside cabinet and grabbed some pain killers from the top. A few seconds later he clambered out of bed and rushed towards the kitchen to get a glass of water. Within twenty four hours, his life had been ripped to pieces and everything he loved and depended on had been stripped away from him. The heartless nature of the invisible force that destroyed it, had spared him no mercy or compassion and as he absorbed the empty shell that his life had now become Genesis sighed in defeat. Life had conquered him and there had been simply nothing he could do to stop it. He quickly swallowed the painkillers and then sought solace in the most soothing medication he knew as he poured himself a glass of whisky and slipped in some chunks of ice. The cool liquid drizzled down the back of his throat as he sat down quietly on the sofa in the lounge and mourned.

Unfortunately, the day seemed to have begun already without him and as Genesis glanced quickly at the clock on the wall nearby. He shook his head as he realized, he'd actually missed the morning entirely. He'd woken up very late and the day oblivious to his heart break had simply carried on without him, it cared little for his presence or his absence, he quietly concluded. He drank some more whisky and sighed as he realized abruptly, the time today was now actually an irrelevant entity as he had no job that required him to be present at a certain time and no other appointments to attend to. There was just a simple nothing.

A few minutes later Genesis stood up and made his way to the bathroom as he forced himself to participate in the day and world. He began to shower and dress as he contemplated how he would actually spend the rest of his day and what he would actually do with the abundance of free time that he now had. He'd go out he decided rapidly lounging around the house alone would simply make him feel more depressed than he already was. He quickly checked his bank balance on his phone to make sure the money promised to him had actually been put into his account as his ex-employer had said it would be, it was there and that slightly appeased his broken heart and relieved a few worries that had been occupying his mind. At least he wouldn't be heartbroken, jobless and totally broke, just heartbroken and jobless. The rest of that day he quickly decided, he'd spend in a drunken stupor in a bar somewhere. It was far too early he thought, to actually attempt to pick up the pieces of his broken life and face the obstacles that finding another job involved or even another lover.

At least Genesis concluded, he wouldn't have to worry about money for a while, the redundancy payment would more than cover the bills for a few months as he wasn't a wild spender. Now that Cherise had actually gone, Genesis realized he actually had one less expensive overhead to maintain. Cherise was beautiful and lovely but she'd definitely cost him an arm and a leg as he tried to maintain her expectations and expensive tastes. She was very high maintenance and there was absolutely no denying it and Genesis knew, he'd struggled at times to give her the kind of treats and comforts she was used to enjoying.

The engagement ring box, sat on the table in the lounge silently as Genesis glanced at it briefly for a moment. He picked it up, opened it and admired the ring inside it for a few seconds as he contemplated what should have been. The ring was pretty and elegant and it sparkled as daylight shone into the lounge through the nearby window as the particles of light bounced of it blissfully ignorant regarding the misery the ring had actually induced.

Cherise hadn't wanted it, she'd rejected it, she'd rejected him and the coldness of that rejection made Genesis shiver as he quickly snapped the box shut and thought about taking it back to the shop. He put the ring box inside his trouser pocket, grabbed his car and house keys and phone from the lounge table and prepared to leave. The shop might reimburse him with something he thought. He'd return the ring that very same day, he quickly decided. Any money he received from doing so might come in handy once the redundancy payment he'd been given ran out. Finding another job might actually be possible at some point in the future but Genesis simply couldn't predict when that would actually happen and the money and ring were all he had to keep him afloat until it actually did.

Being unemployed was quite simply, just not something Genesis was used to. He'd worked for the same company for years and hadn't even thought about moving around or seeking another position elsewhere. Genesis had sought work straight after completion of his degree and had only ever worked for two employers, both of which he'd been with faithfully for years. To be unemployed, unwanted and rejected made him feel useless.

The lounge today was unusually tidy Genesis observed as he glanced around the room quickly. He wasn't the tidiest or most organized of people but recently he'd hired a cleaner to come in twice a week and she'd brought some kind of order to the chaos that usually adorned his home. The result of his decision had been amazingly refreshing and now the house was remarkably clean in comparison to the usual upheaval he somehow managed to reside in and the usual layer of dust that lay over all his belongings had totally disappeared. The cleaner who had actually been hired in an attempt to impress Cherise had also been employed to actually convince her after their engagement to move in with him.

"I have a cleaner now. They come in twice a week." Genesis had explained to Cherise just a week before his dismal attempt at a marriage proposal. Inside he'd hoped that his commitment to the cleaner would also convince her of his commitment to her and their future together. "The house is very tidy now."

"Wow that's a great help Genesis. Do you pay them?" Cherise had asked curiously as they'd sat in the eatery he'd taken her to for lunch.

"I do." Genesis replied.

Hiring a cleaner was an effort that Genesis had made which actually had much deeper implications than simply hiring someone to clean his home, he'd actually wanted to show Cherise that he didn't simply view women that he had relationships with as just some kind of domestic help or cleaner. Cherise who had actually visited his apartment many times prior to the employment of the cleaner, had often commented on the chaotic nature of his disorganized home. When Genesis had actually asked Cherise to move in with him he'd wanted to avoid her thinking that perhaps somehow she would have to be responsible for cleaning up and organizing that mess and that had meant, the cleaner had been an urgent necessity. His home was decorated in simple colors with brilliant, shiny white walls and adorned with simple dark, brown wooden and leather furniture, it was nothing special to write home about, but it suited him. If one day Genesis actually met a woman that was willing to have children with him, he knew he'd have to change the color scheme drastically as it was likely that any child that lived there would stick dirty hands all over the walls and ruin the fresh, white glean. It was unreasonable to expect them not to.

The bar Genesis selected as a suitable venue to accommodate the drunken stupor he intended to wallow in was empty as he arrived and entered inside. He sat down quietly on a bar stool next to the bar and glanced at a food menu lying on top of it as he contemplated quickly whether he should actually eat something first or not. The landlady stood behind the bar quietly as she waited to serve him whilst he browsed. A few seconds later Genesis nodded at her as he surrendered to his appetite and quickly picked out a simple burger dish with fries and ordered a whisky to accompany it from the landlady who by this time had approached him and now stood facing him.

"I'll have a burger with fries and a whisky please." Genesis said politely as he glanced up at her.

"Such a strong drink so early in the day." The landlady teased playfully as she picked up a bottle of whisky from behind the counter and started to pour the murky, brown liquid into a glass. "What went wrong? Women troubles? Work?"

The question she asked prompted a smile to appear on Genesis's face as he realized how obvious his troubles were and how his choice in drink had divulged his mood and exposed the heartbreak he nursed, quietly inside himself. The landlady, a large framed lady in her mid-fifties, smiled glad to see that he'd perked up a little as Genesis allowed a brief grin to cross his face for a few seconds.

"Unfortunately both." Genesis replied. "And at the same time."

The landlady nodded as she put the glass filled with whisky down in front of him and then plonked two ice cubes into it, that she'd plucked out of an ice bucket from underneath the bar. "Give me two minutes please." She explained. "I'm just going to go organize your meal."

Genesis nodded and reached for his wallet as the Landlady disappeared through a door at the other end of the bar, a door which he presumed led to the kitchen. She arrived back behind the bar about five minutes later, armed with a plate of piping hot food and put the plate down on the bar in front of him as Genesis smiled and handed her twenty dollars.

"Better to drink on a full stomach." The landlady advised him as she smiled and picked up the money from the top of the bar.

Jazz music wafted gently into Genesis's ears from the speakers nearby almost as if each note floated on a particle of air as it drifted towards him and penetrated his ear drums. He started to eat hungrily, surprised by how hungry he actually was as the aroma of the food tickled and tantalized his senses. Due to the distraction of the migraine he'd felt when he'd woken up earlier that day, he hadn't even given a single thought to food or his stomach, until he'd actually arrived inside the bar and seen the food menu. Now however as the pleasant aroma from the plate in front of him wafted into his nostrils and teased his hunger, he surrendered to his appetite as he scooped up mouthfuls of food eagerly and shoveled them into his mouth in an attempt to satisfy the sudden pangs of hunger running rampant through his stomach. Life would continue he thought, once he'd healed from the recent pains, it would take a while but it would definitely continue.

The landlady bustled away busily behind the bar as she hummed to the music and attended to some glasses which she cleaned and dried and then stacked on some shelves nearby. She placed some bottles into the refrigerated shelves along the back of the bar as she continued to make light, pleasant conversation with Genesis whilst she worked. Genesis responded to her questions, in-between mouthfuls of food as he appreciated her efforts to reach out to him. Somehow her conversation seemed to normalize his mood as she kept him from slipping down the slippery slope into the abyss of depression, that awaited all to eagerly to consume and engulf him with its arms of misery.

The landlady due to the emptiness of the bar was obviously free to talk to him and didn't mind actually doing so, Genesis concluded. The usual lunch crowd that she'd probably usually entertain, would have been and gone by now he thought as he glanced around him at the empty tables nearby for a moment thoughtfully. The dark, mahogany tables and chairs were all vacant and abandoned as they stood to attention, laid with utensils that glistened under the bright lights that shone down from the ceiling above them, sparkling and clean as they waited for their next occupants to arrive. The lunch crowd that he'd manage to avoid, would now be firmly seated back behind their desks at their respective jobs Genesis thought, a responsibility that he quite simply no longer had to adhere to. The reality of that was in some respects enjoyable but in other ways deeply hurtful, work to Genesis was a duty that he still wished, he hadn't actually been liberated and freed from.

Once Genesis finished his meal, he quickly drank the whisky that remained in the glass nearby and then ordered another one. The landlady smiled as he paid her and then poured another measure into his glass. She cleared away his plate away and headed back to the kitchen once more as she disappeared through the doorway and left him to his own devices for a few minutes. Whilst she was gone a man in his early fifties entered inside the bar, sat down next to Genesis quietly and waited for the her to return.

"The landlady should be back in a minute or two." Genesis explained politely as he turned to face him. "She's just in the kitchen at the back."

The man nodded appreciatively and then started to make polite conversation as he began to tease Genesis gently. "That's a very stiff drink for this time of day. Is it money troubles or women?" He enquired playfully.

The question he posed made Genesis laugh as he realized very quickly that absolutely everyone understood his problems without him even opening his mouth, just from the drink he'd ordered and the actual time of day it was. They no doubt recognized the desire for a stiff drink with which to drown their sorrows from their own experiences in life and could identify with his state of despair immediately.

"It's both." Genesis replied as he smiled. He raised the glass to his mouth once more and paused. "I lost them both." He took a mouthful of whisky before he continued. "In the very same day."

The man listened to his sorrow filled words as Genesis spoke and then shook his head sympathetically. "It happens, sometimes life goes wrong, things go wrong, sometimes people are wrong." He explained. "Sometimes jobs are wrong for us and so are lovers. Losing something is not always a bad thing. Sometimes in the longer term, even though we don't always see it at first, they're actually really doing us a favor." He continued reassuringly. "What do you do for a living?"

"I was a computer programmer. For five years I worked for the same company." Genesis replied as he glanced at the man somewhat curiously as the wisdom of his words intrigued him and caught his attention.

"Well if you are interested, I actually have a vacancy." The man invited as he responded. "The work's probably a little more experimental than what your used too, but the perks are great and the salary is quite handsome too." The man reached into an inside pocket of the black suit jacket he was wearing as he spoke and plucked out a business card. "Call me on Monday and we'll have a proper meeting." He insisted.

The offer immediately intrigued Genesis as he accepted the card and placed it in his trouser pocket enthusiastically. He drank up the remainder of his whisky and then glanced at this phone for a second as he checked the time, the afternoon was quickly departing and the day was being rapidly consumed as Genesis decided that he should really leave and make his way towards the jewelry shop to return the engagement ring before the evening rush actually commenced. Time was escaping him and Genesis really wanted to avoid the embarrassment of returning the ring he'd bought to the shop in front of too many other customers, customers that would no doubt visit the shop throughout the evening rush on their way home from work.

"I'll do that." Genesis replied gratefully as he prepared to depart.

A few seconds later the landlady actually returned and stood in front of the two men as she faced them and smiled. She greeted the man who'd entered the bar. "Nice to see you Caton."

Genesis stood up quickly and smiled at them both. "Thanks so much for everything." He insisted appreciatively. "You both really cheered me up."

"Things will get better soon." The landlady insisted as she encouraged him. "You'll see."

The comment and the smile on her face comforted Genesis as he left an extra twenty dollar tip on the top of the bar and prepared to face the world once more. He walked back out onto the street as thoughts ran through his mind about how perhaps something magical had actually just transpired inside the bar. Perhaps he had somehow been blessed by the gentle hands of a mysterious entity, that perhaps protected people from total and utter despair. By next Monday, Genesis thought as he walked briskly down the street outside the bar, he might actually even have another job. A miracle it seemed, could perhaps occur, he'd walked into that particular bar with no notions of what might actually happen there and he'd actually been offered a job. Perhaps there was a God somewhere out there after all Genesis mused, perhaps someone did care about his broken heart, devastated spirit and crushed soul. Perhaps all the negative things in his life had to be taken away in order to bless him with something more positive, interesting and fulfilling, he contemplated as he arrived at the street where the jewelry shop was situated and walked towards it.

The bar which Genesis had left behind was now quiet as the landlady glanced up at Caton seated on the nearby bar stool and smiled. She poured him a small glass of red wine and then handed it to him.

Caton smiled as he took a sip and then nodded at her. "I think you did the right thing Letty." He said.

Letty leant over the counter towards him as she addressed him. "Thanks for coming straight away Caton. I remembered you said last time you were here, you were looking for someone to work for you and he seemed so disheartened. It would have been such a waste to let him leave without seeing you first.

He was so down, he might have slipped into a hole of despair. I called you straight away."

"He's perfect, just what I need." Caton reassured her as he placed fifty dollars on top of the bar and then quickly stood up and smiled. "Buy yourself something nice to wear."

A few seconds later, Caton departed as Letty smiled appreciatively at his generosity and picked up the fifty dollars from the top of the bar and tucked it away quickly in the front pocket of her apron. Her crystal, blue eyes, quickly skimmed the large interior of the bar as it sought out any potential customers that may have slipped inside the building whilst she'd been distracted by her conversation with Caton, luckily there were none.

The evening rush wasn't actually due to start for another hour or so and that meant, Letty still had time to fix herself a late lunch and relax a little beforehand. She made her way quickly back towards the other end of the bar and then disappeared into the kitchen as she smiled contently. All the world's ails couldn't be totally fixed by her but at least for one person, today, she might have actually made a slight difference she thought.

The ring shop seemed to beckon to Genesis as he approached it, but the closer he actually came to the shop entrance, the more deeply his nerves destabilized him and disturbed his thoughts. He began to feel slightly unsure about what he would actually say to the jeweler inside as he prepared to enter the building. Cherise had dumped him and the thought of how exactly he would explain her rejection to a total stranger, confused him for a moment as he hesitated outside in the street, just outside the shop door. The door opened and a customer walked out, which forced him to immediately walk inside the shop as they politely held the door open for him. Luckily for Genesis the same man who had actually sold him the ring stood behind the counter as he approached it and actually smiled at him to greet him as he drew near.

"How can I help you today? Did the ring fit? Do you need an adjustment or something else perhaps?" The shop attendant asked eagerly.

Genesis paused as silence filled the air between them for a moment before he glanced into his eyes sadly. "I've had a bit of a problem." He said softly as he searched for the courage inside himself to admit the truth. After a short pause, he blurted out the words that sat firmly behind his lips as he pushed them firmly out into the air between them. "My girlfriend, well, well, well, she actually dumped me before I could even give her the ring." He admitted sadly, defeated by the truth of his circumstances.

The shopkeeper paused for a moment thoughtfully as he shook his head, disturbed and saddened by the news. A few seconds later, he nodded as he offered a response, eager to try and accommodate the situation Genesis was now faced with. "Sadly these things happen sometimes. Would you like to return the ring?" He asked.

The look on his face and the tone of his voice were gentle as he smiled at Genesis softly to encourage and reassure him that actually returning the ring, in the circumstances he was in was a perfectly acceptable thing to do. Genesis nodded as he placed the ring box down on the glass counter in front of him and accepted his defeat, Cherise was gone and although he still had the ring, she'd never actually want it or wear it.

"Since it was cut to size and I had to make several special adjustments to it and personalization's, I'll only actually be able to refund you half the amount you paid for it." The jeweler explained.

The solution the jeweler suggested relieved Genesis as he appreciated his accommodating response and nodded in agreement. It was the only real solution available to him and Genesis knew that it would actually take the jeweler a while to sell the ring again, if indeed he ever actually managed to even do so. First he'd have to actually find another buyer who actually wanted it and then the potential buyer would also have to be someone whose needs it aligned with in terms of size.

"That'll be great." Genesis replied as he smiled appreciatively.

Although the actual style of the ring was beautiful and would attract many potential buyers, Genesis knew the reality was every woman had different sized fingers and that Cherise's fingers were extremely slim, which was unusual. That factor would definitely have an impact on how quickly the jeweler would be able to resell the ring and it would definitely take him a while to actually sell it again as very few women actually had fingers that were that slim. The offer he'd made to Genesis was reasonable and made total sense as he quickly accepted it and accepted the financial loss. The partial refund, Genesis might need to provide a financial cushion and to protect him from any potential financial difficulties he may or may not face in the near future due to his recent job loss, pushing the jeweler for more money he quickly decided wasn't wise and may actually put the offer he'd made in jeopardy.

The jeweler picked up the ring box, opened it and inspected the ring, which he found was in perfect condition as Cherise hadn't actually even worn it, not even for a second. He quickly touched a screen nearby, situated on top of the glass counter case that contained many sparkling items of jewelry inside and started to process a bank transfer to transfer money back into Genesis's bank account. Once the transaction was complete Genesis bade the jeweler farewell and departed quickly, anxious to leave due to the humiliating nature of his visit. He comforted himself a little as he left the shop as he contemplated the kindness that the jeweler had shown towards him, although being dumped by Cherise had been an horribly, embarrassing experience in many ways, at least the financial costs of that horrible event had now been slightly reduced.

The street outside was quiet as Genesis walked along it as the evening rush had not yet erupted and spilled out from the offices and stores nearby. He thought about Cherise as he walked. Cherise actually had someone waiting in the wings for her as she had actually cheated on him, whilst he on the other hand, had no one. He hadn't kept any potential love interests on the side just in case things didn't work out, he'd invested all his emotions into their relationship and now he was paying the emotional price as he spent his evenings and nights alone, nursing the abruptness of Cherise's rejection and departure. At least the ring had gone now, Genesis thought as he consoled himself with the knowledge that now there would be one less reminder of Cherise inside his home.

That weekend seemed to pass fairly quickly as Monday arrived and greeted Genesis enthusiastically as it embraced the morning eagerly full of warmth and joy. The bright sunshine flooded in through his bedroom window as warm hues shone onto his duvet and woke him up bright and early. The rest of his weekend had been slightly chaotic as he'd entertained himself by visiting a few bars, unlike the previous week however, he'd actually resisted the urge to get absolutely, leglessly drunk as he'd done straight after Cherise's departure. He'd managed to satisfy himself with fewer drinks and comforted himself with the thought that Monday may usher in a more promising future as he'd curbed his alcohol intake. The sunshine and warmth outside however could not totally lift his spirits as he arose and glanced out of the window with a glum expression. Genesis absolutely loathed being unemployed, it made him feel helpless and useless and his current circumstances dampened his mood. The words of his mother echoed through his ears as he stood by the window quietly.

"What good is it to spend your life doing nothing?" His mother had once asked him during one of her advice sessions in his younger years. "If you're capable of working, it's a good way to keep you busy and out of trouble."

The thought of his mother prompted a smile to appear on Genesis's face as he turned and walked towards his closet, he picked out some clothes and laid them out on top of his bed carefully in anticipation that there may actually be an interview or meeting later that day with Caton. He wouldn't call his mother or go to see his parents right now he thought, not until he'd fixed all the problems. His parents had actually met Cherise a few times and although his mother didn't seem to really like her, she was growing increasingly anxious about Genesis's need to marry and settle down and had begun to pressure him to make a commitment to her. His mother he thought, would now be even more devastated, if she actually found out Cherise had dumped him just as he was about to propose to her. That news, Genesis decided, would definitely upset her. He'd keep the news of Cherise's departure to himself for a while and that way she wouldn't worry, he quickly decided. His mother always worried about him and the recent series of events he knew, would simply heighten the concerns she felt and push them right off the Richter scale. He'd keep his pain to himself for now and carry it alone on his broad shoulders.

The previous night as Genesis had laid in bed and prepared to sleep, he'd speculated further as to the nature of the job he might be applying for the next day but had eventually given up as there were no real clues to what it might actually be as Caton had not provided him any. He'd finally managed to satisfy himself with the thought, that whatever surprises Caton had in store for him, he'd discover the next morning as he'd surrendered to tiredness, void of any real answers and drifted off into a deep sleep. Unlike the night right after he'd lost his job however, the previous night he'd actually been able to sleep quite peacefully as sleep had embraced him and the thought of Monday morning had comforted him. He hadn't tossed and turned, disturbed by his broken heart and lack of employment.

Excitement began to flow through Genesis's body and his skin tingled as the time of discovery surrounding the mystery job offer, approached. He quickly ironed his trousers and shirt and then hung them up on the wardrobe door nearby and then glanced down at his wristwatch. The business card he'd been provided with was as mysterious and intriguing as the owner that had actually handed it to him he thought as he held it in his hands for a few moments and studied it further quietly. The name of the man who'd actually given it to him, Caton was clearly displayed on the center of the card in large gold and black lettering alongside a few phone numbers and an email address. Even his name was unique, intriguing and mysterious, Genesis thought as he clung onto the business card tightly.

The job on offer had not yet been fully explained to Genesis but he was slightly hopeful that it might be something more interesting than his prior engagement at the technology company, Redford Systems Inc. Although he'd worked there for years and been quite content, the daily sales targets he had to meet and routine tasks which simply involved satisfying customer's problems had become slightly boring and presented little in terms of a challenge to his intelligent mind.

Luckily Cherise he thought, actually had no idea that he'd lost his job and been made redundant just after she'd actually dumped him. Thankfully she was unaware that he'd actually suffered another humiliation on top of the one she'd already delivered. If he'd lost his job before Cherise had actually dumped him he concluded, that probably would have pushed her to dump him even more quickly. Genesis dressed up quickly and then made his way into the lounge as he paced the room and waited for time to pass impatiently. Cherise was materialistic and there was absolutely no denying it and she'd often even admitted that herself, there was simply no way in hell, she'd have accepted him in a jobless state and he knew it.

"I just like the finer things in life." Cherise would often remark as she'd often dragged him along to fashion shows, luxury holiday locations and lavish, expensive restaurants.

Genesis had simply footed the extravagant bills obediently with no complaints, obligated by her choice to actually be his girlfriend and in total admiration and awe of her beauty. He felt indebted to her presence, simply because she was stunningly beautiful and way prettier than any other woman he'd ever dated in his entire life, up until that point in time. Some of his girlfriend's prior to Cherise had been quite attractive but not cosmetically beautiful like she was and all his former lovers, hung in the shadows of inadequacy as they sat on the memory shelves inside his brain as inferior life experiences in comparison. His relationship with Cherise had perhaps changed him he thought, perhaps now he actually expected more from women in terms of beauty. Perhaps this change to his perception and standards was negative and superficial and perhaps it would ultimately have a negative impact on his future Genesis speculated. It created a false expectation within him, that perhaps he would absolutely never be able to fulfill again. Genesis sat down on the sofa in the lounge as he glanced at his watch again and continued to analyze the impact on his life of Cherise's departure. Perhaps Cherise had created a false standard inside of him that he would never again actually be able to match.

Beauty was as Genesis knew a very subjective issue but most people he'd introduced Cherise too had commented on her beauty and her modelling contracts had actually confirmed to him and everyone around her, that she was indeed very cosmetically beautiful. Was beauty actually the most important thing he asked himself, he'd have to adjust he thought, change his expectations and eradicate those high superficial standards from his mind, it simply wasn't fair for another woman to have to live up to the shadow of Cherise's existence or her absence. At the end of the day Cherise had actually dumped him and not actually married him at all, which meant she had never really been his and nor was her beauty. He had never actually won over her heart or her beautiful face.

The alarm on Genesis's phone sounded out through the air as he quickly turned his attention towards it and focused on the task at hand as he pushed thoughts of Cherise firmly out of his mind. Today he had to prepare for the beginning of a new job, a new opportunity and a new life without Cherise, today Cherise wasn't his priority. Genesis rubbed his hands together as he began to look forward to the phone call to Caton that he would soon make, whatever surprises Caton had in store for him and whatever job he was going to be offered, he was definitely eager to discover more about. His phone lay in his hands as he prepared himself mentally for the phone call he was about to make, the phone call which may change his entire life, direction and future. Life would definitely continue without Cherise.

The business card Caton had given him sat firmly in his other hand as excitement bubbled inside him, he held himself back slightly for a moment as he resisted the urge to call. The allocated, scheduled time for his phone call had not quite arrived yet and was still five minutes away. He'd planned to call Caton at exactly 11 a.m. and the precise moment of his planned phone call had not yet arrived. To call Caton prior to the scheduled, planned time Genesis felt was not advisable, it would perhaps catch him off guard and he might not be available to speak freely. He would call him at 11 a.m. precisely.

On Monday mornings at work Genesis understood, people usually liked to arrive at and settle in a bit before they actually got caught up in any unscheduled activities. Genesis was not part of Caton's usual daily workload, he'd been a last minute addition to his Monday morning and that meant Genesis was actually an unscheduled activity. Hence his phone call would be made in the middle of the morning, not first thing.

ADAPTATIONS

Thoughts continued to chomp away inside Genesis's mind as he held himself back from making the call a few minutes longer, his body almost felt as if it had a restless horse inside of it that chomped away at a bit in its mouth and scratched the ground with its hooves impatiently, eager to gallop away into the distance and progress with a new journey of life. He'd make the call soon he thought as he glanced at his wristwatch once more. Very soon.

MIND ALTERATIONS

The allocated time to make the phone call to Caton finally arrived as Genesis eagerly reached for his phone and prepared to enter the number on the business card that he held in his hands. A few words, a conversation and perhaps an appointment that might change his life forever, loomed on the horizon of possibilities and hope, where the labyrinth of perhaps would take him was uncertain but Genesis savored every moment as he visualized tantalizing, delicious destinations and a much brighter future. He held the phone in his hand and dialed Caton's number carefully. It was early enough on Monday morning to seem enthusiastic and create a good impression, but not so early that it could possibly be inconvenient.

Caton answered the call after only two rings. "Hi Genesis. So nice to hear from you. Can you make it today, later this afternoon perhaps?" Caton asked. "Say around 2 p.m.?"

"Sure I can make it then." Genesis replied enthusiastically as he smiled.

"Great you already have the address, it's on the business card I gave you." Caton explained.

A few minutes later the call ended and Genesis quickly stood up as excitement surged through his veins. He made his way back towards the bedroom to dress in preparation for the appointment ahead quickly and splashed on a dash of his favorite, lucky aftershave. It wasn't that he was superstitious but the aftershave gave him confidence and after the blows he'd recently received, confidence was definitely something he needed every drop off. Although the actual meeting between the two men wasn't actually for another few hours, Genesis was anxious to prepare himself thoroughly as he quickly ran through questions in his mind that Caton might pose throughout his interview. Technically this was a job interview and not a casual gathering of friends and the implications of that pushed him to prepare more thoroughly. He thought of some appropriate responses to potential questions that Caton might ask as he dressed up quickly and then glanced in the mirror on his closet door. Once satisfied with his appearance, he quickly made his way towards the kitchen to fix some lunch. Hunger was definitely lurking in his stomach as it demanded his attention and rumbled like thunder. Genesis quickly prepared a sandwich as he contemplated what they day ahead might actually bring, he wasn't much of a cook but at least he could fix a sandwich without doing too much damage to the rest of the world. A sandwich was simple, it avoided the possibility of burnt offerings that may hamper the rest of his day and would fill the gap sufficiently until later that afternoon, once his meeting with Caton had actually finished.

A couple of hours later, Genesis arrived outside the office building address on the business card that Caton had provided him with. The bricks were a reddish brown and it had four floors that rose up into the air and he smiled as he absorbed it's modern, corporate presence. It was nice to actually be entering inside a corporate environment once more and especially one that might offer him potential employment. He quickly found the entrance, and then pushed open the large, clear, glass doors, full of hope as he stepped inside the building. Once inside the reception area, Genesis quickly found a moderately, attractive female receptionist in her mid-thirties seated behind a large, black, glossy reception desk. She immediately stood up and greeted him enthusiastically as she stretched out a hand towards him. Genesis smiled as he reciprocated her effort and shook her hand gently but firmly.

"I have an appointment with Caton Marshall." Genesis explained. "I'm Genesis Galaway."

"Hi Genesis very nice to meet you. Caton's been expecting you." The receptionist replied. "I'll let him know you're here." She continued as she sat back down behind her desk for a moment and touched a screen in front of her. "Take a seat on the sofa over there whilst your waiting." She continued as she pointed to a nearby sofa situated against the wall.

Genesis nodded appreciatively and then sat down on the huge, black, shiny, leather sofa, right next to the entrance he'd entered inside just minutes before as he glanced at his surroundings curiously. The orange, black and grey tones of the furniture and walls around him, gave the foyer a modern, vibrant feel and denoted a highly professional environment. The floor underneath his feet was a shiny grey, the walls decorated in a bright, sunrise orange and all of the furniture around him was a striking, jet black with a glossy, shiny finish. The contrasting tones seemed to compliment each other as Genesis admired them and contemplated how elegant they were. The wait prompted him to speculate further about the vacancy he was actually being offered and what it could possibly be as he waited with eager anticipation for Caton to arrive. A few minutes later a glass door behind the reception area opened and Caton entered the reception. He noticed Genesis seated on the sofa immediately and smiled at him.

"So glad you could make it." Caton remarked as he approached Genesis and stretched out a hand towards him. "Please follow me."

ADAPTATIONS

It took Genesis just a few seconds to participate with his request as he quickly stood up and reciprocated Caton's gesture. Genesis was ready and very willing as unemployment to him was not a desirable lifestyle choice and Caton held the key to changing his current status and his future. He shook his hand and obediently followed him back towards the glass door he'd appeared out of just a minute before enthusiastically. The two men walked towards the rear of the building as Caton led him through the glass door and then down a long hallway. At the end of the hallway was a glossy, white door with a small, circular mirror at the top, that appeared to be locked. There was some kind of security scanner on the wall beside the door and Caton stood in front of it for a few seconds as it scanned his eye. A few seconds later the door in front of them swished open as Caton turned to face Genesis and smiled.

"This is my office." Caton explained proudly. "Come on in."

The two men entered inside the vast expanse situated behind the door as Genesis stepped inside delicately and Caton followed him a couple of steps behind. Once inside the huge room, Caton led Genesis towards a nearby desk with two black, leather chairs situated at each side as the door shut behind them automatically.

"Please sit down." Caton offered as he pointed towards one of the leather chairs nearby and nodded politely.

The large office had a huge board table situated at one end and several huge, wafer thin screens that clung to the walls around the room as if they were wallpaper. A vast array of high tech equipment ran along one wall and Genesis immediately felt in awe of his surroundings as he sat down quietly. Some of the equipment inside Caton's office, he quickly realized was top of the range, items he'd never even had a chance to ever see before in real life let alone have an opportunity to work with. Genesis swallowed a little nervously as he digested the contents of Caton's office and wondered where and how, he could possibly fit into to the corporate vision he actually had.

"I manage most of my operations from here." Caton explained as he sat down behind his desk. "It's the heart of the company." He touched a screen in front of him and one of the large, wafer thin screens on one of the nearby walls lit up instantly. "Now Genesis I'll explain a little more to you about what our company actually does and what you'll be doing day to day, then we'll touch on your salary, your role and what I expect from you." Caton continued as he leant towards him.

Genesis nodded eagerly as he listened and glanced at the screen on the wall nearby as he watched some info graphics and human images appear.

"We provide a personal service to people in that we enhance their skills, personalities and adapt their abilities according to their requirements and requests. Sometimes we apply logical changes to their minds in order to prompt physical changes to occur within their bodies, however that's a slightly more complex topic." Caton explained as he stood up and walked over to the screen nearby. "Our objective is simple, we enable people to live the life, they actually want to live. I would like you Genesis, to work for us as a People Adapter. You'll be able to utilize your technical expertise to build and enhance our system and you'll also actually provide some services to our clientele."

The explanation provided to him almost blew Genesis's thoughts into mid-air as they somersaulted around the passages of his mind wildly. Whatever he'd expected this earthquake of information that Caton had actually delivered was way off the Richter scale. His eyes widened as surprise grasped him, until they were so huge they almost felt like plates as his eyelids struggled to contain them. The reality of the work actually being done here by Caton's company was absolutely astounding and quite simply something Genesis had simply never, ever heard of before. Not only was he in awe of Caton's equipment now, he was in total owe of Caton himself, the company he'd actually formed and the innovative work that he had pioneered.

"What we're actually doing here Genesis is ground breaking work." Caton remarked. "You will be paid accordingly, however our work is strictly confidential and you'll be expected to adhere to several confidentiality agreements. For the first year of your employment, your remuneration will be two hundred thousand dollars. In the second year that will increase to five hundred thousand dollars, if you meet your objectives and targets in year one, which I expect you will." He continued.

The figures Caton presented, impressed Genesis as he struggled to hide his surprise. Genesis was pleasantly astounded and the more Caton actually divulged his plans to him, the more deeply surprised he was by their contents. Whatever Genesis had expected it certainly wasn't this.

"You may have to work some weekends and evenings. Some of our clients make appointments that are not always compatible with the usual nine to five time working week." Caton explained. "But you'll never have to work more than a fifty hour week."

The final remark, although it implied working hours that exceeded the usual forty hours Genesis was used to, didn't actually bother Genesis much as he accepted Caton's conditions. Right now, Genesis didn't actually mind working weekends and evenings, due to his empty, destroyed social life that had become practically nonexistent ever since Cherise's departure. The few male friend's he retained, he met with very rarely as they all had serious partners and relationships they were committed too and their weekend and evening schedules tended to revolve around satisfying those. Whenever he did actually receive those rare, occasional invitations from his male friends, he would usually participate but as the years had gone by and his circle of friends matured, those invitations had become more and more scarce. The only other weekend and evening outings that Genesis usually participated in on a regular basis were to see his family, who would insist on visits and outings at times. His parents were not demanding however and that meant it would be easy to schedule those around any work commitments.

"What do you say Genesis are you interested in coming on board?" Caton pressed as he urged him for an answer and commitment immediately.

"Definitely." Genesis replied as he nodded enthusiastically. "When do I start?"

"You can start next Monday." Caton replied decisively as he arose from the chair behind his desk. "Great now that's settled, I'll show you to your consultation room so you can have a look around." He insisted. "We're a quite close knit company with only thirty employees at the moment. Once my work becomes more established however, I'm hoping to expand and open branches all over the world."

Caton waited for Genesis to stand up before he headed towards another door situated at the back of his office and Genesis quickly followed him. They both exited the room through the smoked glass door that led into a small enclosure which had an elevator inside it. The door leading into the elevator was open and Caton stepped inside and then beckoned towards Genesis as he encouraged him to follow him inside.

"This is my private elevator." Caton said proudly as the door swished closed behind them. "First floor please." He commanded as the elevator started to move upwards. "Don't worry there's actually another elevator further down the hall to the right of the reception for everyone else." He explained. "This one just helps me get round the building faster."

A few seconds later the elevator arrived at the first floor and the doors immediately swished open, the two men stepped out onto a landing. Just a few meters in front of them at the end of a short passageway that led directly from the elevator, they were greeted by another closed door. Caton quickly guided

Genesis through the door, which he unlocked via another eye scanner situated at the side of the doorway and the two men entered into another larger landing.

"Security is very tight here at New Minds Inc. as we don't want to enable or encourage burglars." Caton explained as they walked further out into the larger landing and the security door swished closed behind them.

The larger landing the two men entered into had three small hallways in front of them that led off from it and Caton quickly headed towards the hallway in the middle as Genesis followed him a few steps behind. They arrived at another door seconds later and Caton unlocked it as he utilized another eye scanner on the wall next to it.

"I'll add your eye print to the security systems on Monday." Caton explained. "So that you can actually access your consultation room by yourself."

The two men entered inside the room as Genesis listened to Caton and nodded politely at regular intervals. The vast space and sheer size of the room struck Genesis immediately as he glanced around the room in total disbelief. He'd never been allocated a space this size to work from ever before and he was totally stunned. There were two huge, wafer thin screens situated on two of the walls inside the consultation room and Genesis approached one and touched it with delight. He walked over towards the desk and touched the computer system situated on top of it gently as he smiled. The system he could see immediately was a hybrid system, state of the art, cutting edge technology and the matt black casing that contained it with flashing red, light trimmings was instantly recognizable. The trimmings shone brightly and turned blue as Caton touched the smaller, wafer thin screen situated on top of the desk and the large screens on the wall instantly illuminated in unison.

"Our clients spend a lot of money on our services Genesis. It's very important that you understand we're not actually here to judge them, just to give them what they want and what they've have paid for with a smile." Caton explained as he glanced up and looked into Genesis's eyes intently for a a few seconds. "We're not God Genesis. We're just granting a few wishes in order to make people's lives slightly more enjoyable."

The explanation Caton provided made total sense to Genesis, who felt that he'd just been blessed by the granting of a few wishes himself. He continued to explore the contents of the room as he listened, everything Genesis could possibly imagine needing was situated inside that room and he was totally delighted. There was a small kitchenette, a fridge, a coffee machine, an ensuite shower and bathroom, a long flat couch like capsule, a huge lavish desk and even a small, board meeting table with chairs at one end. An alcove at one side of the room had three large server systems tucked away inside it and huge luxurious, black, leather chairs surrounded both his desk and the meeting table. It was luxury that Genesis was quite simply not used to, which meant it actually took him some time to absorb his surroundings and to accept that this would be his new working environment. Genesis had to adapt his mind to accept the reality of what he was actually being offered. The new job and the new working location being offered to him had completely taken him by surprise and had far exceeded any expectations he may have had in the run up to his appointment with Caton. There was no job that Genesis could actually imagine being employed to do now, that could actually exceed what Caton had just offered him.

"When you want lunch you can simply order what you want from the menu on the system, the kitchen staff will prepare it and then send it up to you." Caton explained as he opened a hatch nearby with a shelf inside.

The splendor of Genesis's surroundings were breathtaking as he reflected upon and visualized his previous job and the cubicle partition office space he'd been allocated and worked from for years. There was quite simply no comparison what he was being offered here was totally magnificent and he knew it. The whole package Caton had offered him now made his last position of employment seem insignificant and a pale substitute for this glorious manifestation of what work could actually be. Genesis was stunned by Caton's generosity towards his employees as the reality of what he was being offered sank in to his mind like a warm ripple of joy.

"One last thing." Caton mentioned as he started to led Genesis back towards the door. "Work attire, I expect a formal approach, no need for a tie but definitely a shirt and trousers at all times. Although I'm flexible about some things." He continued. "Dress code simply isn't one of them. I like my staff to look professional at all times. It presents the right kind of image of New Minds Inc. to our clients."

Clothing policies were not something Genesis cared much about and that was an issue Genesis was definitely not going to dispute further. Caton's request made total sense to him as he accepted it immediately with a nod and smile. He was used to wearing corporate clothing and therefore it didn't present much of an issue for him. His wardrobe at home was adorned adequately with a range of suits, shirts, trousers and even ties, that came in a variety of colors and shades and he also possessed many long, smart coats for the harsh winter weather. For the salary Caton would be paying him, Genesis was willing to attend work in a brown sack, if he was asked to.

Once Caton had finished his tour, he led Genesis back downstairs via the main elevator and back towards the reception area. They entered through another glass door and Caton smiled at the receptionist as they approached her desk. He proceeded to brief her as to what exactly would happen the next Monday when Genesis returned to actually start work.

"Genesis will be joining our team on Monday Gemma." Caton explained. "Please make sure you message security and ask them to provide him with the relevant access to the systems and areas of the building he'll need to facilitate." He continued. "You will also need to notify the kitchen staff so that they can provide meals for him too."

"Certainly Caton." Gemma replied as she nodded. She turned to face Genesis and smiled at him enthusiastically. "Welcome on board."

Satisfied that everything was under control and that the interview meeting with Genesis had been a success, Caton prepared to leave and return to his office. He turned to face Genesis and stretched out a hand towards him. The two men shook hands as Caton gripped Genesis's hand firmly in his and then released it.

"I'll see you on Monday." Caton clarified as he prepared to depart.

"Definitely. I'll be looking forward to it." Genesis replied eagerly as he smiled.

A few seconds later Caton disappeared through the glass doors once more that led to his office as he left Genesis alone in the reception with Gemma. She smiled at Genesis politely as he prepared to depart as he bid farewell. Once he'd actually left the building Genesis quickly made his way towards the parking lot where his car was parked filled with excitement, it almost felt as if he was floating on the air with each step he took. The positive thoughts ran through the passages of his mind like bright rays of sunshine as he contemplated how he would actually spend the next week whilst waiting to begin his dream job. Now his free time was no longer a vast space unoccupied and unlimited, now once more he would have the responsibility that work provided and duties to attend to. Once more his life would actually mean something.

The next day arrived quickly as Genesis decided to distract himself with a short break whilst he waited, a week was a long time when you had nothing to do. He would go away for a few days and occupy his time, before he was due to actually start his new job. The few days he spent away would provide him with time to relax and an escape from the busy, bustling, throbbing city that surged with people that he lived in. It would give him time to prepare himself for the most exciting challenge of his life and time to enjoy being pampered for a few days after all the disappointments he'd faced in recent times. He quickly picked out a luxury four day break at a five star hotel and booked it as he sat in the lounge and ate his breakfast. The trip since it was a last minute booking meant he actually had to leave later that day and he smiled as he touched the screen in front of him to reserve it. Once he'd paid for the holiday, he quickly prepared to leave as he made his way to the bedroom, grabbed a shoulder bag and stuffed a few items of clothing and toiletries inside it. The trip was quite costly but the price seemed irrelevant and immaterial to Genesis now as he indulged in the lavish expense without hesitation. The remuneration Genesis would now actually be earning, excited him and his usual prudent nature became slightly immune to the costly, impulsive expenditure the booking had actually required as he'd totally ignored it. The new job justified a splurge of cash to celebrate, he'd decided.

The flight Genesis had actually reserved a seat on, was due to leave later that afternoon which meant he could relax a little before he actually had to start making his way towards the airport later that day. A few days break would be good for him, Genesis decided. The trip would distract him from the loneliness he felt due to the absence of Cherise and her abrupt departure as she'd flown out of his life on the plane of betrayal, firmly seated on the wings and in the arms of a mysterious rival, he'd never even had a chance to meet. Genesis missed not having that special person in his life anymore, that significant other to confide in and share news with about the events in his life, he'd been robbed of that joy by a thief that had stolen Cherise's heart by stealth. He still had his parents to confide in but Genesis knew deep down, that simply wasn't the same. He yearned for the intimacy that a romantic relationship provided and that special someone once more, that he could converse with about anything and everything his heart desired. The thief who had stolen Cherise had robbed him of that joy, that luxury and that comfort which he'd become used to and there nothing had been put in its place to console him. There was no substitute that could replace the warmth of Cherise's companionship, only the emptiness of unrequited love, that dwelt within a heart that had been shunned, spurned and ripped out of the ribcage of stability, torn away from the relationship that usually nurtured and protected its existence.

When Genesis actually arrived at the island resort he'd chosen for his short break later that afternoon it was all he'd hoped it would be as he stepped out of the airport and a beautiful landscape greeted him. The leaves of the palm trees situated outside the airport, glistened gently as the sun soaked them with it's warm rays. A driver collected Genesis and quickly whisked him away as he drove him straight to the luxurious hotel he'd chosen. For four days Genesis knew, he would be pampered and spoilt by his hosts and given the luxury treat, after all the recent heartbreak he'd been through, he rightly deserved. Once Genesis arrived at the hotel, he entered inside the foyer and found a short, mature, heavy set man in his fifties waiting for guests to arrive. The mature porter scurried over to meet Genesis and quickly checked his reservation details. He smiled and then quickly took his bags and indicated that Genesis should follow him. Genesis obediently did so as the porter led him down a crisp, brilliant, white hallway nearby, adorned with a plush, dark, grey carpet that sank as his feet stepped into it. The door that led into his suite was a dark, jet, black and the porter unlocked it politely as he flashed the key card over the lock and the door swung open.

The porter smiled and wheeled Genesis's suitcase inside the large suite and then turned to face him. "This is your suite." The porter remarked politely as Genesis towered over him.

"Thank you." Genesis replied as he plucked two twenty dollar bills out of his wallet and handed it to the porter appreciatively.

"Enjoy your stay." The man replied as he accepted the tip and tucked it quickly away inside the dark, grey jacket of the uniform he wore. "The restaurant downstairs is open twenty four hours a day and there's a program guide for scheduled activities, it lets you know when and where they're going to be held." He explained as he pointed towards a glossy brochure situated on a black, glass coffee table nearby. "You can eat meals in your room or eat downstairs. It's entirely up to you."

The explanations complete the porter handed him a key card and then departed as he left Genesis alone to explore his suite. There would perhaps by now be other guests waiting for his attention in the foyer, hence Genesis understood his abrupt departure. The suite door swished closed and Genesis rubbed his hands together excitedly as he walked over to the coffee table and started to browse through the brochure situated upon it. The expectations of what this short break would include were relatively high as it had cost an arm and a leg and the activities he'd seen on the advertisements had sounded promising. He quickly flicked through the brochure and found that most of the things he'd expected to see were immediately visible. A spa massage, which had appealed to him immensely prior to booking the break could actually be requested at any time of the day up until midnight. Genesis smiled as he prepared to indulge in a quick spa and massage before dinner. He touched a small screen situated next to the brochure to access the hotel activity booking system and put in an immediate request.

The spa center itself was situated in a small adjoining building that could be reached through a hallway that led off from the main hotel reception and Genesis quickly made his way towards the entrance of the small building eagerly. Some small signs had been placed throughout the hotel and at the entrance of each hallway that actually directed guests to any part of the hotel and its various facilities they required, which meant it was fairly easy for Genesis to identify the correct hallway to take and he arrived at his required destination relatively quickly. Once Genesis entered inside the small building, he immediately found an attractive woman inside the reception area.

She smiled at him as she stood behind a high, white, glossy bar like structure. "Come for a spa and massage?" She asked politely as he entered.

"Yes." Genesis replied. "I'm staying in the executive suite. My name's Genesis Galaway."

"Ah yes. You just booked in. Yes I can see you've booked a session." She confirmed as she glanced at a screen situated on top of the white, glossy bar and touched it. "If you'd like to come with me please."

ADAPTATIONS

The woman who appeared to be in her mid-thirties, had brown ringlets, green eyes and plump pink lips that adorned her face gently and suited her perfectly. She wore a crisp, sparkling white clean, cotton uniform that reminded Genesis a little of a nurses outfit but that was slightly more glamorous. He followed her out of the reception area as she led him towards a small massage room situated further down a hallway behind the bar like desk. Genesis tried to relax as he prepared for the first time since his breakup with Cherise, to actually be touched by the hands of another woman that definitely wasn't Cherise. For so long, he'd only actually ever allowed the hands of Cherise to touch his naked skin and he'd cherished keeping his body for her hands only and even after her departure he'd still remained faithful to her, though he had no idea why he'd actually done so. Now however, that status was about to change and a stranger, a female was actually going to touch his body and massage his skin. The thought of being nearly naked and being touched by another woman for a moment seemed a little strange, a little foreign and a little nerve wracking as he considered it. If a male masseur had actually been allocated to him, a man instead of a woman, Genesis knew deep inside he definitely wouldn't feel so nervous about the massage that was about to take place.

They entered inside a small massage room as the woman smiled at Genesis politely and prompted him to undress. She handed him a white, cotton robe that she'd plucked off a hanger inside a small closet next to the door.

"You get undressed and I'll be back in a few minutes." She remarked as she prepared to leave the room. "Don't worry you'll be perfectly fine." She continued almost as if she sensed his nervousness. "I massage a lot of people. It's just a body you know, a bit of skin and a bit of muscle. Nothing to be ashamed of or worried about."

The masseur quickly departed and left Genesis to his own devices as he glanced around the room and absorbed his surroundings. There was a small wooden, bamboo like structure at the foot of the room which Genesis assumed immediately was the spa and a long bed like couch in the center of the room, where he assumed he would receive his massage. He quickly undressed and prepared for the masseur's return as he slipped on the robe. A thought suddenly struck Genesis as he changed as he realized that the masseur hadn't actually told him her name and that since he'd actually arrived at the hotel, no one else had either. The staff at the hotel had simply provided him with the services he'd required and it was almost as if somehow their names weren't important. He definitely wanted to know the masseur's name he thought. A woman would actually be putting her hands on his naked skin in a manner that to Genesis was quite sensual and he would also be exposing his naked flesh to her as part of the activity. These were all very intimate factors to him and factors that demanded that, he should actually know what her name was before she actually proceeded to do so.

A few minutes later there was a knock at the brown, bamboo like door as the masseur returned to attend to Genesis and actually provide the services he'd requested. Genesis by now was dressed in the robe she'd provided and he smiled as he opened the door and faced her. He stepped aside politely as she entered the room once more and shut the door behind her. She walked towards a small, bamboo cupboard nearby and started to prepare the things she would actually need for the spa and massage as Genesis waited quietly. She plucked some small tubes of cream and bottles of fluid out of the bamboo cabinet as Genesis made light conversation, to break the awkward silence between them.

"What's your name?" Genesis asked her.

"I'm Melinda." She replied politely. "Which would you like first the spa or the massage"

The question Melinda posed threw Genesis off balance for a moment as he contemplated further exactly what each activity would involve and which he should actually do first. "I think I'll go for the spa first." Genesis replied after a short pause.

"Great I'll get that ready for you now." Melinda confirmed as she quickly made her way towards the small wooden, bamboo like structure at the rear of the room and disappeared inside it with some of the bottles of fluid. She reappeared a few minutes later. "Everything's ready for you." Melinda explained. "You can either have a spa naked or there's a towel inside that you can actually wrap around your waist if you prefer. It's entirely up to you." She continued.

ADAPTATIONS

The thought of actually being naked in such close proximity to such an attractive woman pulled at Genesis's thoughts playfully as he contemplated further for a moment, what he should actually do. He shook his head gently as he stood up, walked over towards the wooden, bamboo structure and then stepped inside. He'd definitely wear a towel, he quickly decided. Melinda was a professional masseur, providing a professional service and although the thought of being naked around her was very tempting as she was a very attractive woman, it was simply too much of a temptation for Genesis himself to carry right now. His flesh would definitely struggle to resist any urges which may arise as a result and right now he simply couldn't handle it.

Once Genesis was inside the bamboo spa area, he closed the door and removed his robe and then quickly wrapped the white towel around his waist. He sat down on a nearby bamboo bench and then closed his eyes as the searing heat began to infiltrate his pores. The steam wisped up into the air around him as it completely filled the small bamboo room until he could hardly see the door anymore. The waves of heat lapped against his skin as he leant back against the wall, shut his eyes and wished for a moment that Cherise was there beside him. She would have appreciated a break like this, the luxury the hotel provided and the beautiful island it was actually situated upon, instead however, he'd had to venture there alone and now another woman was actually about to touch the body that had once been saved only for Cherise's hands. The whole trip was in essence a bitter sweet experience for Genesis, that should have been so very different. Cherise should have been by his side.

After twenty minutes inside the spa Genesis decided that he'd actually enjoyed it as much as he possibly could as he stood up, slipped the robe back on over the towel he wore and then made his way back out towards the larger massage room once more.

"Ready for your massage now" Melinda asked cheerfully as she smiled at him.

Genesis nodded.

"Lie down on the bed face down." She explained as she pointed towards the massage bed in the center of the room. "You can keep the towel on, but there's no need for the robe." She insisted.

ADAPTATIONS

He followed her instructions obediently as excitement tingled through his veins whilst a massage wasn't a purely sexual activity, it was a very sensual one and the presence of the very attractive, female masseur had actually aroused him slightly. Genesis closed his eyes as he waited for the massage to start and Melinda's hands to touch his skin.

The massage began and Genesis started to enjoy the warmth of her touch, it seemed comforting, reassuring and extremely tantalizing as she ran her hands over his flesh. His body continued to tingle as she started to massage his muscles more deeply. Her hands seemed to touch every part of his exposed, bare flesh as he relaxed peacefully. Deep inside him, Genesis longed for her hands to actually be the hands of Cherise or the hands of a woman that was ready, willing and available to satisfy his sexual urges as she massaged him more vigorously. His mind began to wander and he actually began to imagine satisfying Melinda as he playfully entertained the thought of entering deep inside her. Whether or not the hotel masseurs actually offered this kind of additional service, Genesis was too scared to even contemplate asking as he simply accepted the limits of what was being offered to him at face value.

All too soon the massage ended as Melinda finished her task and then politely dismissed him. "That's all for today I'm afraid, but you can come back for another session at any time during your stay." Melinda insisted. "You can even request me as your masseur and if I'm available, they'll fit you into my schedule." She invited politely.

"Thanks." Genesis replied as he accepted that the massage was now completely over.

Part of him felt slightly disappointed as Melinda left the room and he put his clothes back on, that the sexual arousal that had been stirred with him hadn't actually been fulfilled or satisfied, but he pushed his disappointment to one side and attempted to focus on the more positive effects of his session as he appreciated the fact that his body now did actually feel, slightly more relaxed. A few minutes later he exited the massage room and walked at a leisurely pace back towards the main hotel reception area as he prepared to eat dinner and spend the evening ahead alone. The massage and spa had slightly appeased and comforted him but the thought of eating dinner alone now, detracted slightly from the initial pleasure he'd felt.

The invitation Melinda had extended to him, although enticing was one that Genesis knew, he could not possibly actually indulge or participate in. To experience and enjoy another massage and the intensity of the arousal he'd felt, which he knew would remain unsatisfied, would definitely be a temptation that was quite simply too much to bare. He simply wasn't strong enough to resist or face such temptations, not right now.

One major achievement had been made that day in Genesis's mind as he walked away from the small building and massage room and returned to the main building of the hotel. Genesis had actually taken a very important step in his battle to overcome the heartbreak that Cherise had inflicted upon him so abruptly as he'd actually allowed another woman, that wasn't Cherise, to touch his naked flesh and comfort his broken spirit and that step although it was a small one, was an extremely important step on the road to his recovery after facing the crippling impact of her rejection.

METAMORPHOSIS

The next Monday arrived all too abruptly as Genesis prepared for his first day at work and his new job with excitement. The huge salary he would now be earning, motivated him to arrive early as he showered, dressed and then quickly left the house with about an hour to spare for his journey. Although New Minds Inc. was actually situated just twenty minutes' drive away from where Genesis actually lived, he wanted to be sure that he would arrive on time and create a good impression on his very first day. His first week at work Caton had already explained to him at their initial meeting, would be spent training and he would spend most of it with the two other people adapters situated on the same floor as he was in the adjacent consultation rooms to his. Throughout his first week, Caton had also explained he'd work basic nine to five hours and the transfer of the two thousand dollars Caton had promised him for living expenses until he received his first salary payment had already been paid into his bank account. The appearance of the lump sum over the weekend had comforted Genesis as it fully reimbursed him for the cost of the short break he'd just splurged some of his savings upon.

The back streets were quiet as Genesis drove along them as he made his way through the city and began to speculate whether or not Cherise might have actually stayed with him if he'd actually been offered this job earlier on in their relationship. It was entirely possible that she would have stayed, but then again it was also entirely possible that she would have still left, he quickly concluded after some deliberation. Women he thought as he drove, were such a strange but captivating paradox. You wanted to love them and make them happy, yet somehow, sometimes whilst doing so you ultimately lost them. Romance made absolutely no sense sometimes.

Once Genesis arrived at New Minds Inc. he parked his car in the private parking lot and made his way quickly inside the building. The receptionist Gemma greeted him as he entered inside the reception with a friendly smile.

"Great you're here and you're early. We weren't expecting you for another twenty minutes. I'll call Edgar to come down and get you." Gemma said as she welcomed him. "Take a seat for a minute please."

"Thank you." Genesis replied

He sat down on the sofa next to the entrance quietly as his mind began to wander back to thoughts of Cherise once more. The beautiful, model who had once been his jewel, had simply dumped him without any warning or care in a five minute conversation and his heart was still nursing it's wounds. He'd been totally confused by her departure as there had been no signs of unhappiness, discontent or complaints up until that point in time, regarding their relationship. In Genesis's mind they had been a happy couple, a happy couple that were just one step away from the altar. Her departure had been a bitter pill to swallow and Genesis even now still faced moments where the lump of rejection stuck in his throat, like an obstruction that simply refused to depart, no matter how many times he tried to drink alcohol to drown his sorrows and wash it away.

A few minutes later Edgar arrived and interrupted his thoughts as Genesis stood up and prepared to greet him. Edgar like Genesis was in his mid-thirties. He had jet, black hair and soft brown eyes. His frame was quite square and bulky and he was a lot shorter than Genesis, which meant that as he walked towards Genesis and extended his hand towards him and prepared to introduce himself, Genesis actually towered over him.

"Genesis right? I'm Edgar. Great to meet you. Glad you're joining our ranks." Edgar remarked enthusiastically. "I'll take you up to my consultation room and we'll get started. You'll be with me today and on Wednesday, Kane tomorrow and on Thursday and then on Friday, you'll spend the day with Caton, according to the schedule he's prepared for you."

Genesis nodded as he listened.

"Don't worry about a thing, we'll show you the ropes and how things work around here." Edgar insisted. "Help get you started." He placed his arm gently on Genesis's back as he spoke and led him towards an exit situated at the right of the reception desk as the glass doors in front of them swished open.

The hallway they entered into led immediately towards an elevator and as they approached it, the doors opened and they stepped inside. Luckily Genesis had prepared breakfast at home that morning before he'd left home and that meant that his morning would be pretty straight forward with no interruptions for food breaks. He'd known in advance that his first week would be spent entirely under the supervision of other people and had no desire to inconvenience anyone by requesting any mid-morning breaks to fill his stomach.

"First floor." Edgar instructed as the elevator doors closed abruptly behind them.

Not even a second had passed before the elevator started to move upwards rapidly and just a few seconds later the doors swished open again as the two men stepped out into a hallway. Edgar quickly led Genesis towards his consultation room as he started to divulge a few more details to him about how their day together would actually be spent.

"We'll be seeing three of my clients today." Edgar explained. "One in the morning and two more in the afternoon. They've requested some adaptations and today I'll be making the adjustments to their minds that they've requested."

Genesis listened quietly and nodded politely as they entered inside Edgar's consultation room. Two chairs were positioned behind his desk and Edgar offered him one and Genesis sat down. He watched Edgar sit down next to him and then touch the screen in front of him as he started to conduct the tasks he had to perform that morning before his first consultation was actually due to begin. He quickly showed Genesis around the basic functions of the system as they waited for his first client to arrive.

"There are three types of mind adaptations." Edgar explained. "Skill impartations, personality attribute enhancements and intellect adjustments." A huge grid appeared on the screen in front of them as he spoke and on the two large, wafer thin, screens situated on the walls nearby.

The consultation room itself Genesis quickly observed was exactly the same as the consultation room Caton had allocated to him in terms of size, equipment, furniture and facilities, although the furniture and adjoining bathroom were in slightly different positions due to differing physical layout of the room. The similarity immediately reassured Genesis that the treatment he was being given by Caton was exactly the same as other people being employed to perform the same job, he had been recruited to perform. Edgar continued to give him a guided tour of the system as he described in more detail the intricacies of the mind adaptations system, which he simply referred to as Adapt as Genesis listened attentively.

Approximately thirty minutes later Edgar was interrupted as his first client arrived and Gemma paged him, her face appeared on the middle of the screen in front of them as she smiled. Genesis was surprised by the appearance of her face but it didn't seem to bother Edgar at all as he simply smiled in response, accepted the page and started to listen to her speak.

"Your client's here." Gemma explained as her voice wafted out into Edgar's consultation room through the speakers in the screen in front of him.

ADAPTATIONS

"Thank you very much Gemma. I'll be right down." Edgar replied politely.

A second later the screen reverted back to the images it had been displaying before the interruption as Gemma ended the call and her face disappeared.

"You can wait here Genesis, I'll be back in a few minutes." Edgar explained as he stood up quickly. "I'm just collecting my client from reception."

Genesis nodded as he watched Edgar leave the room. His mind began to wander as he sat patiently alone waiting and he began to visualize what Edgar's client might actually look like as he waited for them to return. Would they look strange and odd? What kind of people needed adaptations to their minds? Five minutes later his questions were answered as Edgar returned with an attractive brunette in tow, that appeared to be in her late thirties. Edgar smiled at Genesis as they entered inside the room and the woman giggled as she laughed at Edgar's rough attempts at humor and the conversation he'd made prior to their entrance.

Throughout that morning, prior to Edgar's first client's arrival, Genesis had quickly realized that Edgar wasn't a great conversationalist and that he was actually really, quite socially awkward. His attempts at light conversation however to put his client's at ease, seemed to pay off as the brunette embraced them and responded positively. She quickly sat down on a luxurious, black, leather chair situated opposite Genesis and smiled at him. A few seconds passed before she actually stretched out a hand towards him and prepared to introduce herself to him.

"This is Genesis Loretta." Edgar explained as he sat down behind his desk and quickly introduced Genesis to her. "I'm preparing him for his own client list. He's new here so be gentle with him." He teased. He turned to face Genesis and smiled at him. "This is Loretta, Genesis. She's one of my long term clients. We see each other at least once every fortnight. We're practically dating." He teased playfully.

Loretta giggled.

"Nice to meet you Loretta." Genesis said as he smiled at the bubbly brunette, seated in front of him and nodded enthusiastically.

The client session began as Edgar prepared to apply the required personality adaptations to Loretta's mind that she'd asked for. She'd requested a change as she wanted to be more outgoing and seductive than she currently was and Edgar participated fully as he encouraged her to become more adventurous.

"What's the use of being a beautiful woman if you can't enjoy the experience Loretta." Edgar insisted. "I totally understand."

"I'm very good at being platonic friends with people." Loretta explained to them both. "But I don't just want to be seen as friendly. I want to be seen as sexy, exciting, seductive and exhilarating." She continued.

"It's ok Loretta you don't need to justify yourself. I totally get it." Edgar replied. "You want to be a cheetah not a snail." He teased playfully.

The response thrilled Loretta who giggled with glee as she nodded eagerly. Edgar understood her, she thought as she waited for him to load her mind map onto the screen and fine tune her brain through the microchip that had been implanted inside her when she'd attended her very first New Minds Inc. appointment. The microchip itself had simply been implanted through a small prick in her thumb and it had been a simple, painless process. According to the information session, she'd attended prior to signing up the Adapt microchips travelled through each client's body and made their way towards the relevant part of a client's brain within a few days. That had meant that by the time Loretta had actually attended her second appointment at New Minds Inc. the microchip had actually been situated in the correct place and was fully operational. Loretta had simply accepted the small thumb prick graciously and the insertion of the microchip had caused absolutely no discomfort or intrusion to her life and she'd attended her sessions with Edgar ever since.

The mind adaptation was prepared as Edgar touched the screen in front of him a few times and then stood up. He walked around his desk towards her and then gently took her arm as he led her towards a sofa situated nearby that appeared to have some kind of transparent lid above it.

"Come and lie down on my couch for a few minutes and by the time you leave here, you'll be the sexiest woman alive." Edgar teased playfully as the two walked across the room together.

The playful nature of his remarks seemed to amuse Loretta, who giggled again as Genesis smiled. It was becoming quite apparent to Genesis however as he watched and listened to them both as they interacted, that Edgar gave each of his client's an intimate, personal consultation that paid close attention to not only their individual requirements but also their personalities. His approach was not distant, remote or regimented and Genesis began to appreciate how much effort it actually took to achieve such a good rapport with people, that were essentially strangers. Perhaps Edgar wasn't as socially awkward as Genesis had initially assumed. The two quickly reached the long, leather sofa and Loretta jumped straight onto it as Edgar smiled. A few seconds later, he pulled down the capsule like cover that fitted over the top of the long couch as he closed it over her body.

"Now shut your eyes Loretta and dream of good things for a few minutes." Edgar insisted.

Loretta giggled again.

Once Edgar was satisfied that Loretta was securely situated inside the capsule, he walked back towards Genesis and sat down as he touched the screen on his desk. He focused on the screen in front of him intensely for a few seconds as it suddenly filled with a large image of Loretta's brain. A small cursor travelled through the image to a certain point and then stopped as both men watched. The image on the screen in front of them then suddenly magnified as Edgar started to touch the screen again and adjusted some numbers that appeared in front of them.

"Adapt." Edgar explained to Genesis as he worked. "Finds the relevant part of a client's brain according to the instructions you input into it and then you can simply increase or decrease the numbers according to what your client has actually requested to flex their personality attributes. I usually only perform an increase or decrease of up to fifty units either way on any given session for a client." He continued. "Though at times if my client expresses specifically that they want a much more extreme change, I vary it to one hundred units or even at times the lowest and highest limits on the scale." Edgar lowered his voice as he continued to speak. "It really depends on the client, what they actually want to achieve and your own judgment regarding the suitability of their request."

ADAPTATIONS

From his discussion, it started to become evident to Genesis as he listened what exactly his role as a People Adapter would entail and how he would be expected to interact with his own clients. The potential the role presented was a lot more exciting than Genesis's previous job and the various complexities that would arise seemed to be significantly more intellectually challenging than he'd initially envisaged even after his first meeting with Caton. Now Genesis could actually see the system at work and how it actually impacted real human beings minds as he began to understand how much focus and concentration his job would actually require.

Each client he would have attend to, would have their own specific issues which he would have to learn to manage, he'd then have to resolve their problems and actually make decisions about their brains which would have a huge impact on their life and world. Whilst each client chose and controlled what they wanted to some degree, the People Adapter they'd actually been allocated too, he quickly realized ultimately made the final decision and retained an element of control over the whole process. The responsibility that Genesis had accepted, he now realized was actually quite huge in comparison to what he was accustomed to as he considered the possible ramifications of any mistakes he might possibly make. The reality struck him as if it was a huge, cold slab of meat that had been slapped across his face, he was actually going to be really messing around with other people's brains. His job, his work and his clients were not something to be taken lightly and neither was the duty of care he would owe towards those he would be making mind adaptions to. Now Genesis understood why Caton paid People Adapters such a large salary, with such large rewards came a huge amount of responsibility and now he would ultimately bare the weight of that responsibility upon his own shoulders.

"You have to decide what's right for each client." Edgar explained. He lowered his voice as he continued to speak. "At times you might even have to ignore your own instincts and apply the most extreme adjustments, even when you might not be totally sure about doing so. Some clients are very sure about what they want and they become extremely irritated if you attempt to undermine their express requests." He whispered.

Genesis nodded as he listened quietly and processed everything that Edgar had explained to him. Finding the balance between client desires and his own judgment would be tricky at times he quickly concluded and that would possibly be the area that would present him with the most problems.

"Things do get easier the more often you see a client." Edgar explained. "You start to understand their preferences, lifestyle and objectives and then you can usually predict what will satisfy them the most." He pointed towards the screen as he spoke and Genesis leant towards it attentively as he continued. "As you can see Genesis, I'm actually making her personality slightly more extroverted by increasing the levels in the personality components that impact on her boldness, confidence and sensuality. There are around one hundred and twenty different personality attributes that you can actually modify to achieve the results a client wants. Skill enhancements are usually slightly easier in that we simply upload a skills file and tweak it to the level of ability that the client has actually requested. For intellect adjustments which are usually enhancements, we usually increase the client's memory, logical reasoning abilities and pattern recognition skills. Again, if a request is regarding a particular field of knowledge, we simply upload an expert knowledge file related to the particular area they've requested, straight into their brain once their intellectual capacity has actually been increased."

Once Edgar was satisfied that his explanations to Genesis were sufficient and that he'd covered all the relevant topics, he quickly turned his attention back towards Loretta once more, who was still lying quietly inside the capsule couch nearby as he touched the screen in front of him. Edgar quickly started to perform the adjustments that Loretta had actually requested for that session as he focused on the screen in front of him intensely. A few minutes later he turned to face Loretta as he spoke to her and reassured her that her requests were actually now being performed.

"Right Loretta your requests are being processed." Edgar exclaimed loudly as he touched the screen in front of him once more. "Sorry to keep you waiting."

ADAPTATIONS

The words 'PROCESSING PERSONALITY ADAPTATIONS' appeared on the screen in front of them as the pod around Loretta started to shine. A bright, blue light emanated from inside it and seeped out of the edges as it seemed to bubble over and spill out onto the floor as the two men watched.

Loretta giggled.

A minute later the screen in front of the two men changed as the words 'ADAPTATION COMPLETE' appeared. Edgar smiled and immediately stood up. He walked over towards Loretta as the bright, blue light that surrounded her faded and lifted up the capsule lid, he then helped her sit up as she smiled at him.

"How do you feel Loretta?" Edgar enquired curiously.

"Way more confident already and definitely much more feminine." Loretta explained as she quickly climbed off the couch.

The couch was unusual in the sense that it wasn't like anything Genesis had ever seen before, it was long, cushioned and soft unlike a clinical couch and positioned at around waist height unlike a lounge couch. Possibly Caton had ordered them from a specialist manufacturer that adapted their products according to his needs he thought. Loretta and Edgar walked back towards the desk and sat down as Genesis watched them both quietly. At times throughout the consultation Genesis almost felt a little like a third wheel, in the sense that he was actually an external party to the professional, client relationship that existed between them. He'd tried not to allow this issue to bother him however as the training Caton had organized for him was essential preparation for the position he would actually be stepping into the following week. The two sat back down and smiled at each other as Edgar touched the screen in front of him and prepared to end the session.

"I'll make another appointment to see you again in a week's time." Edgar insisted. "Let me know how things go and how you actually get along with these personality touch ups." He continued.

Amusement lingered on Genesis lips and a gentle smile emerged as he realized that the mind adaptations Edgar had performed to Loretta's mind had actually had an immediate impact. When Loretta had actually walked back towards the desk and sat down, he'd noticed that her hips now swung more to each side with each step she actually took. The exaggeration in her hip movement now differed significantly in comparison to how she'd walked into the room when she'd first arrived, prior to her mind adaptation. The mind adaptations that Edgar had made, had actually worked.

Loretta nodded and smiled sensually at the two men as she stood up and prepared to depart. The mind adaptation she'd just experienced made her feel almost drunk with joy as she started to walk towards the door. Edgar stood up quickly and joined her as he prepared to escort her back down to the reception. Each step Loretta took now felt more enjoyable and it almost felt as if she was walking on sunshine itself as a ray of fresh boldness seemed to fill her body. Electric pings of sensuality seemed to seep through her veins as her body tingled with an unknown, undefined, bubbling wave of pleasure.

"I can feel the change already." Loretta gasped almost breathlessly as excitement quickly overtook her. "I'll call you to make my next appointment on Friday." She insisted. "I have to check my work diary first."

Edgar nodded as they approached the door.

A few seconds later the two disappeared from the room entirely and left Genesis once more alone as he started to digest the events he'd just observed. Genesis was totally impressed. The professionalism and service that Edgar had actually delivered to Loretta was perfect and suited her needs precisely and Genesis hoped deep inside, that he too would actually be able to satisfy his own clients in the same manner. The generous salary he was being rewarded with and Caton's trust and belief in him, demanded total satisfaction from the clients that Genesis would actually be allocated to serve. The first session that Edgar had performed in front of him so perfectly, immediately set a standard for Genesis regarding what he was expected to deliver to every single client he was actually entrusted with at every single session he provided to them.

The change in Loretta's attitude had been totally remarkable and as Genesis had witnessed the metamorphosis that had occurred, right before his very eyes he'd been struck almost dumb by the instant transformation. She'd transitioned into a much more confident, sexually alluring woman much like a caterpillar that sheds its skin and becomes a butterfly and the change had been immediate. There was quite simply no margin of error when it came to actually making adaptions to people's minds and Genesis now understood the real gravity and impact of his involvement. Each client request and session demanded intense depths of concentration and there quite simply was, no getting it wrong.

The rest of the week passed relatively quickly as Genesis interacted with clients belonging to both Edgar and Kane and observed their sessions. He experienced much more regarding the services he would actually perform for his own clients, safely nestled under the other consultants wings as he watched them and assisted them as they attended to their various client's requirements. The technology of the Adapt system by now had intrigued and totally captivated Genesis in that he'd quite simply, never, ever, before seen anything quite like it in his entire life and how the system interacted with the coordinator and clients and performed such complex, intricate, sophisticated adjustments to the brain of a human being completely blew his mind. He had always known as a computer technician that technology had the potential to actually deliver a lot more than it was within the company's he'd actually worked for, but just how much more he'd never actually been certain. Now however he was starting to see that potential realized and was able to admire and participate in some of those more complex possibilities.

The last day of Genesis's first week at New Minds Inc. arrived as Genesis prepared to spend the day with Caton. He arrived outside Caton's office punctually at 9 a.m. as they'd agreed and was briefed as to exactly what the day ahead would entail as Caton greeted him and invited Genesis inside the room. Caton quickly prepared a coffee for Genesis from a small coffee machine situated by the kitchenette area and then prepared to get down to the business of the day as they both sat down at opposite sides of his desk and sipped on the piping, hot, bitter mugs of strong coffee in front of them.

"Today I'll be preparing you for some of the other duties your role entails, the programming aspects." Caton explained. "The other People Adapters are not involved in this side of my business at all, so in that respect you're very unique. However I have taken that into consideration in terms of your salary and you are being paid a bit more for the additional responsibilities. Your client list is also slightly smaller, which will allow you more free time to engage in programming tasks." Caton continued as he smiled. "Raccoon who also works on the programming side will be your main point of contact. You'll be working on development tasks with him. You'll meet him shortly. How are you finding my company so far Genesis? Do you like what you've seen?"

The question prompted a smile to appear on Genesis's face as he responded. "I really love everything so far. It's beyond my wildest dreams in terms of careers and work." He replied. "So interesting. So unique. So challenging. I'm really looking forward to seeing my first clients."

"Great" Caton replied. "That's what I like to hear. So many companies these days are so monotonous, they offer little in terms of variety to employees. I like my employees to feel fully engaged and to realize their full potential, whilst pleasing our clients. It's very important to me."

A few seconds later Caton touched a screen in front of him and the office door behind Genesis swished open and he quickly turned to face it as a man in his early fifties entered the room. His grey and black speckled hair was relatively sparse and he was quite tall and lean in stature. He quickly approached Caton's desk and smiled at both men.

Caton quickly rose to his feet. "This Genesis is Raccoon." He explained. "As I mentioned he'll be working with you on some technical projects."

Several questions immediately entered into Genesis's mind as he stood up quickly and stretched out his hand towards the man who'd just entered. Why was he called Raccoon, was that really his real name and should he actually address him that way or was it strictly a name that Caton called him? The questions sat firmly behind his lips however as he dared not release them into the air to be heard by any other human being aside from himself. His offer of a handshake was reciprocated immediately as Raccoon leant towards him and grabbed his hand with both hands. The firmness of his grip caught Genesis off guard slightly for a moment and surprised him as he contemplated how such a lean looking man could actually be that physically strong. Genesis smiled at him and began to contemplate what might actually happen next as he remained silent.

The plan for the morning ahead was discussed as Raccoon sat down beside Genesis and faced Caton. Before their departure, Raccoon agreed what time exactly he would return later that day and bring Genesis back to Caton's office for his final briefing. The final briefing which would prepare Genesis for his own client list, the following week. After the short discussion had concluded Raccoon led Genesis out of the room and back towards the reception area once more. They then headed down another long hallway to the left of the reception and passed a few closed doors before they finally reached some stairs that led down towards a basement area.

"I have the whole basement to myself." Raccoon boasted as he walked down a few steps. "It's nice and quiet. I get a lot of work done."

"Is your name really Raccoon?" Genesis dared to ask as soon as Raccoon engaged him in light discussion.

Raccoon laughed. "Nope but everyone calls me that. My real name is Zachariah." He explained as he continued to lead Genesis further down the stairs. "People just call me Raccoon as it's a bit of mouthful. They also say I can find gems of nourishment amongst the garbage as sometimes I retrieve important things when the People Adapters have done things wrong. I restore files they've messed up and save their lives before Caton finds out." He teased. "So they nicknamed me Raccoon. It's kind of joke really."

The stairs twisted round in a kind of spiral and when they reached the bottom, they were immediately faced with a black, metal, strong looking locked door. An optical eye scanner was situated on the wall next to the door and Raccoon stood in front of it as it scanned his eye print and the door unlocked. The door swished open a few seconds later and the two men entered inside Raccoon's secret basement area.

"What you are about to see, experience and work with, within this area of the building is totally confidential Genesis." Raccoon explained as they walked through the doorway. "Absolutely no one is allowed into this area besides Caton and myself. You have now also been given access, but this access is not to be taken for granted." He continued as he led Genesis through a small reception like room and out into a larger, circular doom like room at the opposite end.

In the second dome like room was a huge structure, situated on a circular platform in the middle of the room, a small platform led out towards the structure and all around the platform was a deep abyss that seemed unending. Raccoon led Genesis out along the small platform towards the structure in the center of the room as Genesis glanced down into the deep darkness below curiously, he couldn't see the ground below him at all. The structure itself was shaped almost like a 3D cube and it seemed to have some harnesses inside it. Genesis stared at it curiously as they approached whilst he speculated quietly inside himself as to what exactly it could possibly be.

"I'll strap you into Adapt and give you a little tour so that you can see and understand the kind of technology you'll be working with."

Raccoon explained politely as he stepped inside the cube and beckoned towards Genesis to follow him.

The cube itself seemed to compose of millions of tiny fragments, that glistened and sparkled as small glimmers of light from some small, bright lights that clung to the walls around the dome like room bounced off them. Whatever it was and whatever it was made from was totally beyond Genesis's comprehension as he participated with Raccoon's request and stepped inside the cube. The various harness straps were then quickly wound around him before Raccoon strapped himself into the cube also. Raccoon took two head visors down from a hook just above his head, handed one to Genesis and then put one on himself. Once the head visor was positioned over his eyes Genesis immediately noticed that the lens in front of him made the room look quite strange as it displayed a warped view of his surroundings and seemed to serve no purpose that he could visibly see.

"Do we really need these?" Genesis asked Raccoon politely.

"Definitely." Raccoon replied. "Wait a minute and you'll find out why."

A few seconds later the cube started to move as it span around and around and Genesis's body jolted in surprise as it adjusted to the unexpected movement. The walls of the room around them started to change as they disappeared and Genesis and Raccoon entered into the Adapt system through the backdoor as a female voice sounded out into the quiet darkness that surrounded them.

"Hello Raccoon. How can I assist you today?" The female voice asked politely.

"Hello Adapt. I'd like to check on the upgrades I made last week to the skills core please." Raccoon explained politely as if Adapt was an actual human being.

Genesis smiled as he listened.

"Certainly Raccoon." Adapt replied.

The still, black darkness around the two men suddenly changed as both Raccoon and Genesis found themselves in a large hallway, the walls of which were adorned with lots of small, electronic drawers. The constraints around their bodies were gone, the dome room walls were gone and so was the cube, they'd actually been situated inside before the female voice had greeted them. Raccoon gently took Genesis's arm and led him to a nearby drawer, he touched it and it lit up immediately and opened. The huge, electronic filing cabinet they seemed to be inside transformed as their surroundings changed once more and Genesis found himself and Raccoon in a studio like room. In the center of the room two people were actually sword fighting, a man and woman and they continued with their battle as Genesis glanced at them curiously.

"What are they doing?" Genesis asked Raccoon as he leant towards him and whispered in his ear. "Can they actually see us?"

"Sure." Raccoon replied quietly. "But they're not human Genesis, so don't expect a human response. They're programs." The man and woman continued to clash swords until Raccoon interrupted them politely. "I installed some new sword fighting techniques last week and I just wanted to know if they are workable and ready for implantation." Raccoon explained as he approached the two sword fighters at the center of the large studio like space.

ADAPTATIONS

The two programs immediately stopped sword fighting and relaxed as they turned to face him. The man nodded to confirm that the new adaptations were ready in response to Raccoon's request for information.

"How did you find them?" Raccoon asked them both curiously. "Any problems?"

The two programs glanced at each other and then shook their heads as they responded to his question.

"Can they actually speak?" Genesis asked curiously as Raccoon returned to his side and led him towards a doorway nearby.

"They can't actually speak, however they can transmit messages through Adapt." Raccoon explained. "That means that if there are actually any problems, Adapt will communicate the error messages through logs directly to me. I think they've finished testing the upgrades now so I should be able to activate the new sword fighting techniques I installed."

"Do you actually create all the new techniques for all the different skills?" Genesis asked curiously.

"Not all of them, some I simply purchase from various specialist software vendors, they usually have to be modified slightly first and then incorporated into the Adapt system. Some however I write and design myself." Raccoon explained. "It can be quite interesting at times, it gives me a chance to develop knowledge about things I would never usually have known anything about."

A few seconds later, the two men found themselves once more back in the electronic filing cabinet hallway with the small electronic drawers inside it once more as Genesis glanced at the walls around him in total awe. Blue lights streamed through the lines that separated each drawer as Genesis contemplated further for a moment, what kind of rooms some of the drawers may actually contain inside them. The long hallway seemed to stretch out into infinity as he screwed up his eyes and attempted to search for an end in both directions. His efforts were futile as the hallway seemed to extend far beyond his own line of vision in both directions and no end could be seen at all.

"This is like a huge filing cabinet." Genesis remarked as he suddenly glanced upwards and quickly realized that he couldn't see the ceiling either, the drawers simply extended upwards in regimented lines that never seemed to end.

"Very huge." Raccoon teased.

"Does it go on forever?" Genesis asked curiously.

"I don't think so. I think it simply repeats itself over and over again kind of like a loop." Raccoon replied. "So no matter how far down the hallway you walk you'll never actually find the end. I didn't design it." He explained. "It was here when I arrived."

The complexity of the Adapt system stunned Genesis as he absorbed his surroundings and admired it more deeply. The system that Caton had actually built was deliciously intelligent, amazingly intuitive and absolutely every computer technician's dream. To work with such a system first hand and be involved in such ground breaking work to Genesis was a total privilege. So often he'd been confined to simply assisting users with problems and selling software that he hardly even believed in, now however he was actually involved with something that was unique, purposeful and that had unlimited potential. It was a breathtaking moment.

"Adapt we'd like to exit please." Raccoon instructed as he addressed the computer system once again.

"Certainly Raccoon." Adapt replied politely.

A few seconds later the two men found themselves strapped back inside the cube once more as they exited the large, filing cabinet type hallway. Raccoon quickly undid their constraints and Genesis slipped the head visor off and handed it back to him.

"Adapt is so deliciously complex." Genesis remarked stunned by the sheer complexity of the Adapt system itself. "How on earth did someone design all this?" He enquired curiously, flabbergasted by the deeply elaborate structure of the system that provided the framework for the modifications he would actually be performing on actual human minds.

"They say Caton and five other scientists designed the system." Raccoon explained as he stepped back out onto the platform that led out of the dome shaped room. "He's not just a pretty face you know." Raccoon teased as he lowered his voice slightly. "The man's actually a total genius."

The two men wandered slowly back down the narrow platform as Genesis digested

Raccoon's words. His explanation somehow made total sense to Genesis who could now finally understand Caton's commitment to his vision. Not only did he manage the company on a daily basis but he had actually formulated it, created it, built it and then kick started it from the crumbs of a few scattered ideas that had existed within his mind. It had taken dedication, discipline, hard work and last but not least an extreme amount of intelligence. The sheer magnitude of Caton's achievement and his abilities suddenly struck Genesis as he began to appreciate and accept that perhaps, he might actually be working for one of the most intelligent human beings alive on the face of the planet.

EXTREME PLEASURES

The next week started and Genesis was eager to please as he looked forward enthusiastically to engaging with his own five clients that Caton had initially assigned to him. He'd been provided with a detailed briefing about each of the clients he'd be meeting that week, during the final briefing the previous Friday afternoon. Caton's instructions to him had been very precise and clear.

"Remember Genesis give your clients exactly what they want. We're not here to judge them, simply to provide a service to them." Caton had emphasized. "Adapt is here to enable clients as human beings to fulfill their unrealized potential so they can realize their hearts desires, to allow them to bask in their passions and participate in their deepest ambitions successfully. He'd insisted. "And if you need any assistance don't be afraid to ask. We don't expect you to be an expert straight away." Caton had said reassuringly as he'd patted him gently on the back as they'd walked towards his office door. "Our clients spend a lot of money on our services, it's important that we satisfy them properly." He'd insisted. "We like to get it right, the very first time."

The explanations provided to him by Caton had been much clearer and more definite than the advice given to him throughout either Edgar or Kane's training sessions. Caton throughout his briefing had made it completely clear and removed any uncertainty that may have existed in Genesis's mind completely, that the client had the ultimate say in their mind adaptations and that his judgment was not to interfere or be applied to the detriment of their enjoyment of the services they had paid for. Since Caton was Genesis's boss and since he actually ran the entire company, Genesis knew instinctively that his instructions were paramount and far superior to any other employee's advice.

The briefing on the Friday afternoon had been quite short and Genesis had been released early from work as he'd embraced the weekend enthusiastically and waited impatiently for the Monday to arrive. Unusually, Genesis now found himself in a position where he actually looked forward to the working week ahead and wanted the weekends to pass more rapidly whereas in the past, throughout his working years it had usually been the other way around and that change was immediately refreshing. The weekend had sauntered by slowly as deep down inside he'd yearned for it to end as he'd looked forward to the Monday ahead. Impatience had now grown inside him as it chomped on the bit of eagerness and urged him to hold the reins of his destiny; he yearned to actually climb into and sit in this exciting, new saddle that his new job would provide as he prepared for the Monday to actually arrive, when he would start to embark on the ride of his life. Edgar, Kane and Raccoon had wet his appetite sufficiently and now Genesis longed to actually hold the actual reins and steer the horse and not just be a spectator.

ADAPTATIONS

That Monday morning as Genesis sat in his consultation room, he prepared for the day ahead as he started to browse through the profiles of his clients on the screen in front of him and analyzed them further. His client group composed of three men and two women. The clients were mostly in their thirties and forties which immediately reassured Genesis and put him at ease, mature people he concluded, usually had a better grasp and understanding about the things they actually wanted in life and they would be less likely to create problematic situations for him. He studied their profile details more intensely as he attempted to learn as much as he could about each person before his first consultation was actually due to start that later that morning.

The first male client, he was due to meet, was called Titus, he was a stock market trader in his early forties. He seemed to be doing exceptionally well financially and Genesis couldn't help but gaze in astonishment at his personal net worth as it appeared on a screen in front of him as he drilled further down into his personal details. He'd paid Caton a huge sum of money on account and Caton as a result was very eager to please him.

"He's one of our biggest clients Genesis." Caton had mentioned at the briefing that previous Friday afternoon. "Make sure he's very happy."

Genesis had understood the implications of his remark immediately. Caton was letting him know very politely, that if Titus asked for cake, he was to be given a cake with a cherry on top. Titus was a client, Genesis simply had to go that extra mile for and there was no debate about that at all. He'd also been allocated another client who fell into that category, she was called Jade and Caton had also paid additional attention to and mentioned her throughout their briefing. These two clients were Genesis's top two clients and the two clients that would spend the most money and they were the two client's Genesis had to ensure he satisfied completely. Luckily Genesis's appointment with Jade wasn't actually scheduled until much later in the week and that gave him time to focus his attention solely on Titus's appointment first.

Gemma paged Genesis from the reception an hour later as Titus arrived. "Your clients here." Gemma announced as her smiling face appeared on the screen in front of him.

"I'm on my way." Genesis replied as he quickly stood up and prepared to make his way downstairs.

A few minutes later when Genesis arrived in the reception area, he found Titus seated on the sofa waiting for him, armed with a coffee that Gemma had kindly provided him with. Genesis walked towards him and smiled and then quickly stretched out a hand towards him as Titus stood up to greet him. He was a slight, built man with jet black, thick wiry hair and his skin was a light beige tone. From his profile, Genesis actually knew that he not only spoke English but also Mandarin. He was extremely handsome and possessed not only rugged good looks but also a shy, but cheeky smile that seemed very charming. Titus flashed a grin at Genesis as they shook hands.

"Hi Titus, I'm your consultant Genesis." Genesis explained politely as he introduced himself.

"Nice to meet you." Titus replied in broad, mid-western accent.

The two men smiled at each other for a moment comfortably as if they were old friends, before Genesis led him through the nearby glass doors and hallway to the right of the reception as they headed towards the elevator. On the way towards Genesis's consultation room, he attempted to engage Titus in light discussion as he'd seen Edgar and Kane do with their clients, to put him at ease.

"How was your weekend?" Genesis asked as they entered inside the elevator.

"Great I made five million dollars for a client late on Friday evening in one trade so I spent the weekend celebrating." Titus explained as he grinned. "Commissions will be good this month."

The comment astounded Genesis as he felt a slight burn of envy inside him for a moment as he analyzed the access to mass wealth that Titus actually had just at his fingertips. Titus lived in another world entirely. Genesis pondered about his own lack of courage for a moment as he speculated as to whether his choice of careers had actually cost him his heart's desire, Cherise. Perhaps if he'd been braver, he could have accumulated a lot of wealth and then kept her in a manner which she would have been reluctant to leave. Perhaps he could have made millions like Titus had. Genesis smiled as they approached the door of his consultation room as he kept thinking about how he could have saved his relationship if only he'd had more wealth. They stood outside the locked consultation room door as Genesis quickly shook himself out of the negative thoughts of what might have been and stood in front of the optical scanner as he prepared to scan his eye. He forced himself to analyze and accept the truth as he rejected the meandering thoughts that had wandered into his mind and attempted to focus on the task in hand, his client Titus.

There had actually been no verification at all that Cherise's dissatisfaction with him or their relationship was actually related to money or his career and he could not be certain that the lack of excitement his working class means provided to lubricate their romance was actually what led her astray and away from his arms. For a second he pondered over the possibility, that perhaps her departure was nothing at all to do with money and that perhaps he'd failed to satisfy her in another area of their relationship. That final thought was even more disturbing than the first as Genesis pushed it firmly out of his mind and rejected it immediately. He scanned his eye print in the retinal scanner and the door of his consultation room swished open immediately. He led Titus inside the room and offered him a chair politely and sat down behind his desk. Titus sat down and they began to discuss his requirements as Genesis touched the screen in front of him.

"What would you actually like to achieve with your mind adaptations Titus?" Genesis asked politely as he turned to face him for a moment.

"I'd like to be more confident with women generally." Titus clarified. "But I'd also like to be more confident in the bedroom." He explained. "Believe it or not I'm incredibly shy."

The honest response was instantly appreciated by Genesis as he admired his frankness and clarity. Titus hadn't beaten around the bush or waffled in an attempt to justify his request, he'd simply laid it out on a plate in a manner that was easily digestible and understandable. He'd dived straight into the heart of the issue and he knew exactly what he wanted and exactly what he was there for.

ADAPTATIONS

"How much more confident and adventurous would you like to be?" Genesis enquired curiously as he began to probe him for more precise details.

"A lot more confident with women and much more adventurous." Titus confirmed. "Due to my conservative upbringing, I find I lack confidence in the bedroom and I think I'm actually quite a boring sexual partner, a bit too conservative. I'd really like to change that. My parents were brought up in a very conservative culture and that meant I was too. It's what they were used too and most of the women I've dated up until now have also been very conservative too. That's made it difficult for me to even attempt to be more adventurous. I want to enjoy different sexual encounters, experience different things. Things I'd usually be too scared to even think about doing." He explained.

The explanation made sense to Genesis as he nodded and quickly led Titus over to the long sofa nearby. Titus climbed up onto it and lay down as Genesis put the capsule lid over his head and then made his way back towards his desk.

"Don't forget to close your eyes." Genesis instructed as he sat down behind his desk once more. "The light is very bright."

Luckily for them both, Titus had already had an Adaptations implant installed into his brain and that was something that Genesis did not have to attend to on his first day alone with his very first client. A few minutes later as Genesis started to process his requests, a bright, blue light shone around the capsule as Genesis increased his confidence by two hundred units and sexual prowess by three hundred units. The increases Genesis made didn't quite reach the upper capacity limit as he'd decided to keep the option of a full optimal increase to full capacity for a later appointment if it was actually required. Whilst he wanted to ensure that Titus was not dissatisfied with the results, he was also slightly worried that an extreme increase may be too much for Titus to control in the shorter term. The flexibility of having room to adjust and apply further increases in the future to each of the two personality traits within Titus's brain, would enable Genesis to apply another increase at a later date, if and when one was requested. It was his first day and his very first client appointment and Genesis was slightly anxious about stretching and changing a client's life in a very extreme manner, when he had little knowledge of what impact that would actually have on their lifestyle in reality and the events that may occur as a result. The changes to Titus's mind would be a learning curve not only for Titus but also for him.

Once Genesis had completed the mind adaptations, he crossed the room, lifted the capsule lid and made his way back to his desk with Titus in tow. The two men sat down and faced each other once more as they discussed when their next appointment would actually occur.

"I can see you again in a week's time if you'd like." Genesis suggested. "That will give you some time to become familiarize yourself with the changes you requested and get used to them, then we can review and discuss any other changes you might feel you want to be made."

The suggestion seemed to please Titus who thanked him and smiled appreciatively. A few minutes later Titus departed as Genesis escorted him back down to the reception and the two men made light conversation as they walked. There was a warm satisfying feeling that ran through Genesis's body as he walked and it was almost as if his blood had become warm water inside a radiator as it seemed to heat his whole exterior. The two men parted at the reception as Titus thanked him and shook his hand.

"Thanks for making that so easy for me." Titus said appreciatively. "I was a little nervous about my appointment before I arrived today."

"It's no problem at all." Genesis insisted. "That's what I'm here for. You have a good week and I'll see you next week. Go easy on the ladies tiger." He teased as he winked at Titus playfully.

Once Titus had departed, Genesis quickly returned to his consultation room and sat down behind his desk once more as he smiled. The first client he'd actually seen had left happy, satisfied and content with the mind adaptations that he, Genesis had provided and it was a moment of achievement for him. He'd actually realized the completion of his first client's request and that knowledge immediately reassured him that this was a job that he could actually perform and that he could actually deliver great results. Caton had been right to employ him Genesis thought happily, he would work hard and make sure he added as much value to his company as he possibly could. Genesis felt extremely grateful to Caton for the opportunity he had provided to him and as he reflected on his first appointment with Titus, he knew deep inside that this was indeed, the perfect job for him.

Throughout the remainder of the afternoon Genesis prepared for the remaining four clients he was to meet later that week as he basked in the glorious satisfaction, his successful appointment with Titus provided. When the end of the day approached, he left work and drove home as he concluded that his very first day in his new position had been a success. His levels of confidence started to grow once more as he embraced his success. Cherise, her secret lover and Mr. Ferdinand his old boss had absolutely obliterated his confidence ever since the horrific day of their attack as they'd dropped bombs of rejection into his life. Genesis had struggled to feel good about himself as a result after they'd nuked his ego and the certainty he'd once carried high in the air as he'd rejoiced about his achievements in life, had been totally shattered as they'd trodden his life into the ground like a piece of dirt, stuck to their shoe that they were desperate to get rid of. Now Genesis had a purpose once more, now life had blessed Genesis with her warm, caring hands and given him something to live and work for. Now Genesis would no longer be mocked by those who had ridiculed him and taken his loyalty for granted.

The rest of the week flew by as Genesis met with the rest of his clients and attended to their various requests. Samantha and Jade intrigued Genesis when he met them as they presented some interesting complexities to him in terms of what they wanted and their motivations raised some very interesting questions within his mind. On the Wednesday afternoon when Genesis first met Samantha, he quickly observed that she was a rather plain looking woman in her late forties as he collected her from the reception area. Her initial requests were simply an intellect upgrade and a knowledge enhancement as she sought to improve her knowledge in a particular scientific field, however there were actually two motives behind her requests that made them slightly more interesting. A neurology

Professor she wanted to impress that she had her eye on and dreamed of capturing by enticing him into a committed relationship and a huge research post she wanted to secure. Samantha was adamant as she explained her position to Genesis, she needed the maximum intellect increase she could possibly have and Genesis obediently complied with her request. He could totally understand empathize with her situation and understood what it was like to be without employment and that despair was something he didn't wish on anyone, especially not a client.

"When will you find out about the research post?" Genesis asked Samantha curiously as they returned back to his desk once her mind adaptations had been processed.

"In about a month." Samantha explained. "Their recruitment processes are usually quite slow they take around a month to make a selection."

"I hope you get it." Genesis replied as he smiled and nodded at her. "I hope you manage to get the Professor to notice you too."

Once Samantha departed, Genesis quickly visited Caton's office to ask him a quick question as throughout his session with

Samantha he'd actually noticed that the light that usually shone blue from inside the capsule lid had on this occasion shone orange instead. This difference had aroused his curiosity but also slightly worried him. He was greeted by Caton as he arrived outside his office and he opened the door immediately. Genesis entered inside, explained why he was there and sat down as Caton smiled at him.

"Intellect adaptations utilize a different part of the brain and the Adapt system." Caton explained as he smiled at the issue Genesis had raised and presented to him. "Next week I'll give you a proper tour of the back end of the Adapt system, with your programming skills and knowledge you might find it interesting."

The special effort and offer that Caton extended to Genesis to actually show him around the system pleased Genesis profusely and when he returned home from work later that day, he was very relaxed and extremely happy. Genesis was by now in total awe of Caton's genius and spending one on one time with him discussing technical areas within the actual system itself, would provide him with a chance to not only understand Caton's business better but to also garner a more intimate comprehension of his highly complex, sophisticated mind.

The Thursday morning greeted Genesis as daylight rushed into the open curtains in his bedroom and forced his eyes to open as the morning pushed him out of bed. Genesis didn't complain as he accepted that the day would now commence and started to prepare for work. Today he would be meeting Jade and he was looking forward to their appointment immensely. Jade, the extremely attractive, extremely wealthy, female client that Caton had allocated to him, had captivated Genesis from the moment he'd set eyes on her profile image on the Adapt system. Although he didn't actually care that much about wealth when it came to women, he did have a soft spot for women that were easy on the eye and very physically attractive. He'd looked forward in eager anticipation to actually meeting her in person as he'd restrained himself throughout the week from glancing at her profile image too often in order to avoid being distracted. She seemed to be a vibrant, socially active socialite who came from a very wealthy family, her face was cosmetically very pretty and her body voluptuous with curves that accentuated her toned, slightly athletic looking frame. He'd been slightly curious regarding what she could possibly want to change about herself however as to Genesis she seemed totally perfect.

"I'd really like to be more sexually exciting." Jade explained a little nervously as she sat at the opposite side of Genesis's desk in his consultation room. "My family have a very religious background and its definitely impacted on me, in terms of how I think. I'd also like to be a bit more ruthless as at the moment well I'm a bit of a doormat." She continued. "My father is the leader of a very large church. A very wealthy church. I need to let go of my inhibitions as I worry too much about what the church thinks of me and the things I do or don't do." She explained politely.

The words Jade spoke intrigued Genesis as he listened to her and analyzed the changes she'd actually requested internally. He would increase her sensuality and confidence levels and then reduce her levels of patience and compassion, he quickly decided. He'd start by amending them by about five hundred units each he thought as he glanced at her current brain profile and noticed that those elements of her personality, were very moderate indeed.

"How different would you like to be and how much of a change would you like to see?" Genesis asked politely as he attempted to clarify her position.

"Very different and as much as you possibly can." Jade insisted in a determined tone of voice.

"No problem." Genesis replied. "That's what I'm here for, to grant your wishes." He teased playfully as he smiled at Jade and gazed into her eyes.

Jade giggled at his remark.

Genesis stood up, walked around his desk and then led her gently by the arm towards the sofa nearby. Unlike his male clients and even his other female client Samantha on this occasion, Genesis actually assisted Jade to climb onto the sofa as he smiled at her. Jade was fast becoming his favorite client already and Genesis knew deep inside, he definitely had a soft spot for her.

"What do I do next?" Jade enquired as she lay down obediently.

The question she posed actually aroused Genesis as he immediately thought about a hundred things she could do and indulged in some quick sexual fantasies inside his mind.

Images started to form as he began to consider various scenarios that could actually occur between them. He explored them more deeply for a moment as his mind delved into the exciting, titillating crevices of sexual desire as he visualized what he could actually possibly do with her body, if only he was presented with the opportunity. He'd make love to her passionately, vigorously and frantically, he thought as tingling passions ran through his flesh. He longed for a moment to caress her, strip her naked and explore every area of her body with his tongue and lips as he gazed at her chest. Her breasts poked out of the top she wore cheekily and exposed a small part of her abundant cleavage as her chest seemed to greet him. He yearned to touch them, suck, lick and caress them but his professionalism restrained him from actually doing so. Jade was a client and that was a huge factor, Genesis could simply not ignore.

"You have to close your eyes." Genesis replied in a slightly deeper, huskier tone as his internal desires overtook his body and gripped his throat.

Jade moved her arm and interrupted his thoughts as the images of the possible sexual entanglements he could engage in with her quickly scurried out of his mind and he focused once more on the task at hand. Genesis shook his head as he crashed back down to earth rapidly.

He forced himself to focus on Jade's request as he blocked the sexual thoughts from his mind and pushed them aside. Although Jade was alluring and captivating, Genesis quickly reminded himself that she was actually there to receive a service not to be lusted after sexually. She was a potential sexual encounter that he could definitely not afford to indulge in or even attempt to approach, he quickly decided. He'd only just lost one job and the thought of getting caught up in a romance with client he'd only just met at his new job, would definitely not be the smartest move right now, no matter how tempting that was and how beautiful she was. The whole situation could become messy, ugly and murky and right now a disgruntled romance gone wrong with a client was the last thing he needed.

Once his first working week was over Genesis sighed with relief as he sat in his consultation room and prepared to go home.

He was very appreciative of his position in that he'd survived, he'd delivered and he hadn't actually let anyone down yet. He'd dipped his toes into the rivers of discovery as he'd explored his first clients and their various issues, each one had been given the relevant mind adaptations they'd requested and he'd attended to their needs enthusiastically and thoroughly. He reflected upon his achievements as he reveled thoughtfully within each one for a few minutes. Genesis was no longer a failure, no longer an unwanted item of waste that lay on the ground discarded by those who had once desired him, those who had simply used whatever they could consume from him and then simply tossed him away when it was no longer convenient for them. Now he actually meant something to someone outside of his own family, someone not just obliged to accept him due to the blood connection they shared.

Genesis prepared to meet with Caton before he left work that Friday evening eagerly as Caton had scheduled a brief meeting with him, before he was due to depart for the weekend. Unlike their previous meetings, Genesis knew this meeting was more of a formality than a prescribed necessity as he approached it enthusiastically and waited for Caton in the reception area. The receptionist Gemma, paged Caton to let him know that Genesis was available at 5 p.m. on the dot as he stood by her desk and waited for Caton to respond. He responded immediately and Genesis walked towards his office as Caton opened the door and invited him inside. Once inside Caton's office Genesis sat down and greeted him with a smile as he prepared to answer any questions that Caton might pose.

"How are you finding things?" Caton asked curiously. "Enjoying the work?"

"Yes I really am. It's the first time I've actually enjoyed a job to be perfectly honest." Genesis confessed. "Usually my workload is kind of dry and rigid."

Caton smiled in response. "Look next week I'll need you to work with Raccoon on Friday so if you can make sure that all your client appointments are scheduled to occur throughout the other days, that'll be absolutely perfect." He explained. "I have a bunch of updates to do to personality adaptations, some skills and knowledge improvements. I'd like you to be present even if you can't actually perform any updates yet yourself. It'll give Raccoon a chance to show you the ropes."

Genesis nodded enthusiastically.

"Great that's everything. You can go enjoy your weekend now." Caton remarked as he dismissed Genesis politely.

The weekend was calling to Genesis who by now felt slightly, joyously, drained after his first week at work as he left Caton's office. His body was adjusting to actually being back in a structured work routine and it had totally worn him out. Although Genesis hadn't lost his last job that long ago, during the break in-between, he'd binged on alcohol often, slept late at night and woken up late in the days and his body had as a result become slightly undisciplined. The new job had meant that he'd actually had to sleep at a reasonable hour, get up early and structure his day once more and the change in routine had tired him. He departed work gratefully as he prepared to make his way home and simply enjoy the rest of his evening resting. There would be no wild outings this weekend, he decided.

When the Saturday morning actually arrived, Genesis decided to visit his parents as now that he actually had a job again he felt he could actually begin to face his mother once more and handle any awkward questions that she might pose regarding Cherise and her absence. The visit was planned for the Saturday afternoon and as Genesis made his way over to his parents' house he began to feel slightly anxious. Throughout the drive he began to rehearse some possible responses he could offer, if his mother actually decided to probe him further regarding the topic of Cherise. Whilst the existence of a new, better paid, exciting job would excite his mother, Genesis knew she would still be dissatisfied with his single status and that she would definitely raise the topic. She usually did. She'd be devastated if she discovered that Cherise had actually dumped him just a hundred meters away from the altar.

Thirty minutes later as Genesis parked his car outside the large, family home that his mother and father occupied, he smoothed his hair into place as he glanced into the small interior car mirror and prepared to enter inside. His skin looked clean and fresh, possibly due to the spa he'd had at the hotel whilst on his short break which seemed to have opened his pores and driven out all the collated dust and grim that at times could make his face look dull and lifeless. Genesis took a deep breath, stepped out of his car and made his way towards the front door as he prepared to break the good news and bad news to the only woman left in the world, that actually really cared about him.

Although some of his male friends were actually married, Genesis knew their wives didn't really count as if their marriage to his friend ended somehow, they would quickly become strangers once more. Strangers that he would probably never, ever even say more than hello to if they ever met again at some point in the future. Sometimes they acted as if they cared but Genesis knew to rely on them for support was not advisable. The women in his male friend's lives were what Genesis considered temporary friends, in that they weren't really his friends and their loyalty and empathy towards him, purely depended on the length and strength of their marriage to the friend of his, they were actually married to. If his male friend put a step wrong and their wife actually dumped them, Genesis knew he would then become in all someone that they actually avoided. His mother on the other hand was always there for him and no matter what happened in her relationships, even the relationship with his father, she would always be his mother and someone he could always turn to and rely on for support. Although her probing questions could be irritating at times, some part of him deep inside, enjoyed the irritation and the fact that he actually had someone who cared enough about him to nag and irritate him about matters, they felt were important.

By the time Genesis had actually parked his car and walked up the narrow stony, walkway that led through the garden towards the large, sandy brick house he'd grown up in, his mother had already opened the door to welcome him. She started to make her way towards him as she approached him with open arms. Genesis smiled as he prepared to embrace her.

"Genesis I've been so worried about you." His mother insisted as she hugged him tightly. "It's been almost a month. You don't call, you don't answer calls, you haven't been to see us. I was about to send out a search party." She continued. "It's just not like you. Why are you avoiding me?" She leant back for a moment as she glanced into his face with a worried expression. "Is everything ok? What's going on? Is Cherise pregnant?"

Usually the question she just posed would have made Genesis laugh, but right now Cherise was still a raw topic and he almost winced as he dug deep inside himself for an appropriate response. He shook his head as his smile became slightly strained. "No mum, Cherise is not pregnant." He replied as he took her arm and gently walked her back towards the front door. "I'll tell you everything." He reassured her. "Once we're inside."

Slightly reassured by Genesis's response, she walked towards the door with him and started to tease him about his skin playfully. "Your skin sure looks crisp and clean. Did you have a facial?"

Genesis laughed. "Not a facial exactly."

"Thank goodness." His mother replied as she inspected his face a little more closely for a few seconds, slightly suspiciously. "I know men these days want to be all fashionable and hygienic and care about their appearance but I'm not so keen on men getting facials." She continued. "It just seems so feminine. So extra."

ADAPTATIONS

The house seemed quiet as they both entered inside and Genesis began to speculate further as to where his father might actually be. That question was soon answered as his father appeared in the hallway that led out from the kitchen nearby and made his way towards them. A stout, tall man with a bald head, in his mid-sixties, Genesis's father was a stern but fair man. He'd raised him to respect himself, respect other people and to respect women he entered into relationships with. He was tough when it came to discipline and regimented when it came to homework, tidiness and mealtimes but he had a soft heart. Dinner had always been the family's evening meal and it was the one meal of the day his father insisted they should always eat together. No matter where Genesis went or what he did as a child, his father was adamant that he should return home every single day of the week at 7 p.m. to eat dinner. His bedroom always had to be organized and clean and it had been inspected every few days throughout his childhood to ensure that it actually was. His father, Genesis thought would be surprised if he actually visited Genesis's home more often and discovered the chaos, disorganized mess he usually lived in.

Each time they came to visit, Genesis would spend the day before just cleaning his home in order to ensure his father felt satisfied that he'd raised a good, clean, tidy son.

Genesis smiled as he contemplated for a second what his father might think if he actually discovered that Genesis had employed a cleaner or how he would react if he found Genesis's home in it's usual, chaotic, disorganized upheaval of mess, when the cleaner wasn't actually around. It wasn't that Genesis was lazy, it was just that he became occupied in other things around him and never actually seemed to get round to tidying up much and the mess and chaos just seemed to grow somehow.

The couple chattered away to him nonstop as he followed them into the kitchen and prepared to eat the late lunch that his mother had prepared for him. No matter what time of the day Genesis visited them, there was always a meal waiting for him when he arrived as his mother felt that he didn't actually eat properly and she would make the extra effort to prepare a meal for him whenever he visited. His father who could actually cook also and whip up some very tasty dishes on the other hand, seemed slightly less bothered about Genesis's dietary intake or the lack of it and rarely prepared a meal for him.

They discussed the new garden shed his father had built and some new wallpaper he'd put up in the lounge for his mother, since Genesis had last visited them as Genesis listened and smiled. He compared their home environment to his work environment as he noticed the stark difference between them both. Where he now worked was exciting, very unique, high tech, elaborate, highly stimulating, fast paced, complex and mentally challenging whereas his parent's home on the other hand was down to earth, predictable, laid back and simple.

The three sat down at the kitchen table as his mother quickly dished up some macaroni bake. Genesis dabbled in some gentle topics of conversation with his father, like the weather and the garden as he started to consume his mother's culinary gift eagerly. He was absolutely starving and there was quite simply nothing in the world like his mother's cooking, the lavish restaurants and small diners he often frequented, couldn't even come close. A few minutes later as his mother sat down and faced him, Genesis prepared to answer the more probing questions he knew would be gnawing away inside her mouth and anxious to depart from it. She had held her tongue and her words but her curiosity couldn't be restrained for much longer and Genesis knew it. His mother wasn't nosy, just caring and that meant at times, she asked some very difficult questions and provided advice that he often actually didn't want to hear.

"So Genesis what's been going on in your life." She asked. "Am I hearing wedding bells in the near future? Should I buy a hat or a brown sack?"

"How's work?" His father asked as he glanced at Genesis's face curiously.

Genesis smiled and nodded as he turned towards his father. "Work is great and I've actually got a new job, it pays a lot more money and it's really interesting. Lots of potential." Genesis explained enthusiastically as he broke the good news first.

Lionel, his father was immediately satisfied as he smiled in response. He'd been worried by the long absence and lack of communication which clearly indicated something was definitely wrong and now at least, he'd been reassured that the wrong, was not work related. It was almost as if a huge weight had been lifted off his mind as he nodded at Genesis to encourage him. Genesis had a job and an income and was not unemployed. He could relax.

Whilst Lionel, his father had been satisfied, Trisha his mother was now situated very far away from the banks of contentment, if work was not the problem that meant something else definitely was and that something must be Cherise. She glanced at him suspiciously. Genesis had avoided the questions she'd posed to him about his relationship and now she'd noticed. Trisha began to shake her head sadly, she'd warned him about Cherise the first time they'd actually met but Genesis had gone full steam ahead and continued to see her. The dislike she actually held inside for Cherise wasn't selfish, she knew her type and could read her immediately. Genesis was no match for Cherise and Trish had felt that she would simply use him and then throw him away like a toy when she was bored of the routine and simple middle class lifestyle he led. She would want more and Genesis would not be able to deliver that more. Sure Genesis would try to keep up with her and provide her with the luxuries she desired but deep down, Trisha knew it would be a struggle. Cherise had expensive tastes and Genesis had limited means and she would never actually marry him. Even if Cherise ever actually did, their marriage would be a short lived one, that would ultimately end in divorce or betrayal. Perhaps Cherise dumped him, Trisha thought as she glanced into Genesis's eyes and attempted to read the thoughts that lay in the mind situated directly behind them. How could Genesis have his heart broken by the very woman Trisha had disliked from the very first moment, she'd actually laid eyes on her. Trisha forced Genesis to provide an answer as she stared at him.

"Okay Genesis what's going on with Cherise?" She demanded.

Her stare locked Genesis to the spot as he felt his mother, pin him down with her very direct question. There would be no escaping the question she'd actually posed now and he knew his only choice was to actually answer it. His mother would not drop the topic until he provided an answer and she would definitely not allow him to distract her or be evasive by wandering onto other topics or by presenting an ambiguous answer. He took a deep breath and started to push the food around his plate a little nervously before he actually attempted to answer her question. This was definitely not going to be a pretty conversation.

"There's no easy way to say this Mum." Genesis replied hesitantly as he gazed into her eyes sadly. "There actually won't be a wedding between Cherise and I ever." He explained. "She left me a few weeks ago, on the very night I was actually going to propose to her."

Silence filled the room as if a bomb had just been dropped, the devastation of his news was apparent immediately as his mother coughed and spluttered. She quickly attempted to adjust to his single status as the visions of grandchildren fled from her mind in a flash. Trisha's heart sank down to the cold, grey, stone tiles on the kitchen floor as she absorbed each of his words. Inside she was devastated and even though she hadn't actually even liked Cherise, Genesis had and he'd invested a respectable amount of time into their relationship. Genesis deserved more than a heartbreak, more than a disappointment and more than a rejection from someone who Trisha felt was a spoilt, lady muck that didn't actually deserve her son.

It was a huge setback, Genesis would first of all actually have to recover, meet someone new and then start dating again. It would take him time to actually establish a serious relationship with someone. These events could happen at any time in the future and that could not actually predicted by anyone, Trisha knew it could actually take Genesis years to find someone serious. The prospects of a marriage that had recently seemed so close had now vanished into thin air and departed abruptly with Cherise's exit. He'd run the race and almost reached the finish line, only to stumble and trip over the rock of Cherise's rejection, whilst the other runners around him rushed past. Trisha's heart mourned for Genesis as she shook her head in disbelief, almost as if she wanted to reject the truth. Her sweet natured son had been dealt a harsh blow from the cruel hands and fingers that had refused to wear the ring of commitment he offered sincerely.

"What's your new job like?" Lionel, his father asked quickly as he attempted to interrupt the difficult conversation and change its direction.

Lionel could sense that both his wife and his son were becoming upset and he had absolutely no desire to delve further into the reasons why Genesis had been dumped, by what seemed to be the woman of his dreams. Whatever had happened, it simply wasn't important now, the positive things in his son's life were and the topic of Cherise simply had to be totally pushed to one side. Whatever had happened between them, now only existed as a painful memory that should not be provoked as it lay in the grave of heartbreak. They didn't need to know why Cherise had gone, simply that she'd gone. Cherise and her discontent were no longer important, Genesis however was and the broken heart he carried inside him as he nursed his pain and accepted his loss was evident as his father attempted to focus on the good news and ignore the bad.

"It's really great dad. I have my own huge consultation room. My very own client list and I do special system upgrades and things. It's very exciting." Genesis explained as he shoveled a large forkful of food into his mouth, swallowed it quickly and then smiled at his mother. "This food's great mum as always."

The afternoon progressed and turned into evening as Genesis visited his father's new shed and admired his handiwork. One day, Genesis thought as he glanced at the shed, perhaps he'd have a wife and family of his own to build a shed for. One day when he met someone who actually, really loved him. When the late evening dusk started to fall Genesis prepared to leave and return to his home as he kissed his mother gently on the cheek and she hugged him. Inside he felt quite satisfied that he'd actually managed to face his mother, answer the questions she'd demanded answers to and faced up to the reality of the disappointing event that had almost devastated him just a few weeks beforehand. Admitting Cherise's departure to someone else although painful, somehow seemed to now make it slightly easier to cope with as his admission seemed to provide some kind of closure to him. His family had now also accepted without too much fuss, that Cherise would never actually return to their world and that she would definitely never actually be Genesis's wife.

ADAPTATIONS

Life wasn't the perfection it had once been anymore in that it had been tarnished by disappointment, betrayal and the harsh brushstrokes of Cherise's rejection, but it was starting to look slightly better for Genesis than it had been. The remaining imperfection was something for the meantime that Genesis knew he would simply have to accept and learn to live as his family accepted his single status and lack of marital commitment and embraced his broken heart. One day he'd find someone who loved him, Genesis thought as he drove back home, one day he'd find someone worth building a shed for.

MORAL NEUTRALITY

The first week at work for Genesis had seemed to last an eternity throughout his training period, the next few weeks however flew by as Genesis started to work with each of his clients. Each week Caton added two or three more new clients as his confidence in Genesis increased, which had a knock on affect and further reinforced Genesis's confidence in himself. His appointment schedule varied as he found some clients would only come in once a month whereas others he would only ever see once or twice and some clients seemed to attend once every few months. The clients that only visited once or twice, never usually made any follow up appointments and simply vanished back into their personal lives and worlds once they had what they wanted. The daily variety of his scheduled client meetings, suited Genesis as it offered and presented new challenges to him each day and week. Deep inside he yearned at times to have a few more clients like Jade but none of his other clients even came close to being similar to her in any capacity. Eye candy was a definite plus to liven up his working day but not many of his clients fitted that requirement.

The research scientist Samantha, he'd initially seen in his first week had successfully been chosen for the coveted research position she'd been pursuing, she was over the moon about it. The situation surrounding the Professor however, who'd sparked her interest hadn't however been fruitful yet and she attended another session to attempt to change her personality once more in order to attract his attention a bit more overtly.

"I'd like to dress in a much more sophisticated manner." Samantha explained as Genesis listened to her at one of their consultations. "I'd like to be a bit more motivated to work out at the gym and improve my figure too." She continued.

Genesis searched the skills and personality database for the relevant adaptations faithfully as Samantha sat and waited patiently. "We'll adjust your levels of confidence and sensuality." Genesis explained as he'd glanced at her face once more. "And we'll also improve your dress sense skills and those three factors combined should all compliment each other and give you the results you desire."

Samantha nodded eagerly as she agreed with his analysis.

"Regarding the gym I think an increase in your body consciousness should really push and motivate you to exercise more and that should resolve that issue for you." He suggested.

"You are extremely good at your job." Samantha observed as she praised his recommendations.

"I like to make sure my clients are satisfied." Genesis remarked as he accepted her compliment graciously.

A few of Genesis's clients that seemed to be overly interested in how personality and mind adaptations could enhance their physical appearance so in that respect, Samantha was not alone. Two months after his initial start date Genesis met Genevieve, a young woman in her early twenties who attended her appointment with her mother in tow.

"I want to win a beauty pageant." Genevieve explained immediately. "I have some stiff competition." She insisted as she displayed some photos of the contestants she would be facing on her phone. "I have to look better than they do."

"This is her dream." Her mother Sandra explained. "Well our dream. "We've been going to the beauty pageants for years. She's only ever been placed second or third. She really needs the crown to get proper advertising modelling contracts."

"I can't actually give you any kind of cosmetic surgery." Genesis had explained as he outlined the limitations of his work to them both.

"Look at her face. She doesn't need cosmetic surgery, her body just needs to be a bit more in shape and a little more graceful. She needs to be a little bit more confident." Sandra insisted. "She's on a very strict diet but she seems to binge on junk food whenever I'm not around. Which doesn't help. I've spent a lot of money on her career and I need some results."

"I'll see what I can do." Genesis replied thoughtfully as he made another appointment for Genevieve on his system. "I'll assess the correct adaptations for her and apply them next week. Let's make an appointment for Thursday."

The two women seated before him nodded as he booked the appointment and prepared to show them out. It was a big ask to put the responsibility of a beauty pageant crown on his head but he wasn't one to run away from a challenge so he accepted the request and prepared himself. The modifications he selected in the end were more simple than he'd originally thought as he increased her confidence and sensuality, reduced her impulsive eating urges and increased her levels of body consciousness. It was amazingly interesting to Genesis that mind adaptations could actually be utilized to enhance a human being's physical appearance and that captivated him slightly.

When the two women attended the next appointment Genesis had made for Genevieve, he applied the adaptations he'd identified as appropriate and they were both delighted with the immediate results. Genevieve couldn't sit down as she strutted around the room eager to explore her the impact of her mind adaptations and show them off to all that were present.

"I definitely stand a chance of winning now." Genevieve had insisted as she'd walked up and down the room as if she was on a catwalk. "Look at my walk Mum isn't it amazing. That Barbie doll Paula doesn't stand a chance against me now."

"She doesn't darling. Your walk is amazing. We'll definitely take the crown this time." Sandra insisted. "Would you like to come to our pageant final, it's next weekend?" She asked as she looked at Genesis. "Genevieve was selected to be one of the ten finalists."

The thought amused Genesis as he considered it further for a moment, there was nothing actually in the rules Caton had stipulated to him that said he couldn't actually accept invitations from clients, Attending the event might provide him with a deeper understanding of such clients in future he thought, the pressures they faced and the obstacles they sought his assistance to overcome as he accepted the invitation graciously and nodded in agreement.

"Here's the address." Sandra instructed as she took out a small card and started to write down the details of the venue for him. "We'll see you there."

Genesis nodded.

"We have to go. I have to make sure Genevieve's outfits are all absolutely ready." Sandra insisted as she glanced at Genevieve. "And you have to practice your walk."

"Mum I really think I need a new bikini for the swimwear round, the one I have just isn't as good as Paula's and she'll look a million dollars and I'll look like a dime standing next to her." Genevieve urged. "If we really want to win the $1m beauty product contract that comes with the crown for Luscious Ladies cosmetic company. I'll definitely need a new bikini."

Sandra nodded as she stood up and prepared to leave the room. "You're right darling. We can't get so close to the finish line and victory just to be let down by a substandard bikini. We'll buy a new one on the way home."

ADAPTATIONS

Genesis was surprised by the huge sum of money and modelling contract being offered as a prize to the pageant as he listened to Sandra. This was more than just a desire to validate one's physical appearance, he thought. Beauty pageants were big business and a career maker for young, attractive, hopefuls. The topic of beauty pageants was totally alien to him and existed in what seemed to be a totally different world than the world he lived in, a world which he was totally unfamiliar with however he could understand the desire Genevieve had inside to achieve and succeed.

The results of Samantha's appointment were extremely positive as she attended her follow up appointment later that week. Genesis was stunned as he collected her from the reception and he hardly even recognized her. The pale, homely, rough looking, unkempt woman whom he'd once describe as slightly nerdy, now looked very attractive. Her body seemed to have a few gentle curves, her hair was immaculate and her nails were now perfectly manicured. The outfit she wore fitted her body and skin complexion perfectly and the package she now presented was indeed totally stunning. The physical changes surprised

Genesis as he absorbed and accepted that the mind adaptations he was implementing really could have an actual impact on a client's external physicality and not just their internal minds.

"Samantha you look amazing, he'll definitely notice you now." Genesis remarked as they walked towards the elevator. "If he doesn't he's definitely blind or gay. How are things going?"

"Well." Samantha explained as she gushed with excitement. "I've actually been out on two dates with Professor Lindford already and he actually asked me."

The two stepped inside the elevator as they made their way towards Genesis's consultation room and he smiled with satisfaction. They arrived outside the room and Genesis opened the door for her as he showed Samantha inside. Genesis had actually made Samantha's dreams come true and given her the things she'd labored fruitlessly for, for years. The satisfaction he felt inside, warmed him pleasantly almost like an internal radiator as he accepted the results of his work.

The beauty pageant final arrived and Genesis true to his word prepared to attend, he was somewhat curious as he attempted to step into and understand a world that was very different from his own, a world he'd never given much thought to before. Perhaps Cherise had attended such events when she was young, he thought as he dressed up that Saturday morning in preparation. He dug out a shirt and tie for the event and made a little extra effort over his own appearance as he suddenly reminded himself that he was actually attending a beauty pageant and if he turned up looking less than his own personal best, people might look at him oddly.

The hotel banqueting hall the final was to be held in was huge and decorated with extravagant decorations and Genesis admired the interior as he stepped inside. Rows of chairs sat behind a judges table and some were already occupied by men and women with personal gadgets in their hands that looked like camera devices and microphones. They must work for the media he assumed as he quietly sat down on a chair at the edge of a row, a few rows away from the stage at the front of the large hall. The banqueting room filled up quickly as parents, relatives, news reporters and judges arrived and sat down.

Sandra suddenly appeared out of a side door nearby and she sought out Genesis quickly and then made her way towards him. "So glad you could make it." She gushed. "The pageant is about to start. I'll be in the back area attending to Genevieve's make up and things so I won't be able to sit out front and watch the pageant with you. She needs all the help I can give her." Sandra leant forward and whispered in Genesis's ear quietly. "Paula Perkins is here and she's armed with a hairstylist and a makeup artist."

Genesis smiled and nodded in understanding. "That's fine. I'll be fine here on my own." He insisted. "I totally understand. Wish Genevieve good luck from me. Though I'm sure she'll be fine and won't need it. She's a beautiful young woman." Genesis remarked as he attempted to reassure Sandra that her efforts would not be futile.

Sandra nodded.

An announcer, a woman in her mid-fifties that looked like she was perhaps a model herself, appeared on stage and approached a microphone. Her hair, makeup and outfit were stunning and Genesis knew immediately, to be accepted in this world, you had to be as cosmetically close to perfection as possible. It was a superficial world but unapologetically so, it sought no justifications, had no concern for those who were not deemed to be beautiful enough to be accepted into its elite royalty and had no desire to compromise the superficial standards it held itself up to.

"Ladies and Gentleman if you would like to take your seats please, the final for Luscious Ladies Beauty Pageant is about to commence." The beautiful, mature announcer said.

The crowd of people within the room obediently sat down in their seats as the female announcer captured their attention immediately as her words echoed around the room. The small groups some of the audience had formed as they talked amongst themselves and waited for the pageant to start, broke up as they separated and quickly sat down. Music started to play gently in the background as Genesis watched the five judges arrive and sit down behind the judge's table. There were no smiles or pleasantries exchanged as the judges prepared for the pageant to begin and it seemed to be a very serious affair as Genesis accepted that this was not going to be a light hearted fun, entertaining afternoon.

The rounds started as the ten contestants filed out of a doorway at the top of the room and strutted around the runway stage that led down towards the judges table. Each of the ten young women looked very serious as they focused on their every movement and presentation intensely. Their smiles although pretty, seemed to be painted onto their faces much like the makeup they wore. Each step was a step that would have an impact on their future and held the key to their victory and the ten young woman involved in the pageant, seemed to understand the gravity of the event and their participation fully.

The rounds continued as the ten young women appeared in a variety of outfits and displayed themselves to the audience. The judges nodded at times and made notes as they watched silently. The final two rounds approached as everyone in the room started to relax slightly and the end of the event loomed on the horizon of the afternoon as it drew closer. The first of the two final rounds was a talent round and the second round would be a questions round and the announcer mentioned this as the audience prepared for something a little more engaging than simply a catwalk display of elaborate clothing, perfect faces and immaculate hair styles.

The afternoon would soon be over Genesis thought with relief, beauty pageants he'd quickly decided were totally not his kind of thing at all. Cherise when they'd been together had possibly saved him from this boredom by not dragging him along to such industry events and now for the first time, he actually began to appreciate that. He couldn't really understand the fascination that some people seemed to hold for such activities but he quickly reminded himself that this was actually a professional event and that this pageant would ultimately actually define and kick start some of the young model's involved, professional careers.

The ten young women appeared on stage together as they prepared for the talent display, each woman had been given thirty seconds to deliver a performance and illustrate their talent to the audience and judges and the round kicked off quickly as the women all sat at the side of the stage and the first contestant sang a song. The singing wasn't great but it was decent and Genesis observed she was actually off key a few times, which prompted slight smiles to appear on the faces of the other contestants as they embraced her shortcomings. The round continued as another six women performed their various talents, until finally Genevieve's turn arrived, she quickly stood up eagerly as soon as her name was called and walked out towards the center of the stage. Unlike three of the women before her who had chosen to sing and a contestant who had actually given a gymnastics display, Genevieve had decided to perform a dance routine. She quickly posed as she prepared for her music to start as she smiled at everyone seated in the audience in front of her. The routine seemed to go very well as she entertained the crowd with sharp, crisp moves and performed the splits at the end and Genesis was relieved. She reminded him a little of a cheerleader as she finished her routine and sat back down at the side of the stage once more.

The first of the final two young women approached the middle of the stage and prepared to perform. Music started to play as she danced, it seemed to be a ballet, classical like routine, that seemed to involve a lot of rolling around the floor. Occasionally she stood up on her toes and lifted one of her legs as she attempted to vary her movements but it was rather dull to watch. Genesis smiled and nodded encouragingly as he watched to avoid being pessimistic however and to ensure he'd didn't knock anyone's confidence. Towards the end of the routine, she lifted her leg and attempted to hold it up against her head when suddenly, there was a splitting sound as her outfit seemed to tear and start falling apart. There was a huge gasp as the audience watched as expressions of shock and horror crossed their faces. The audience, the judges and the contestants all turned and stared at the young woman in the center of the stage. She crumbled into a heap on the floor, totally defeated by the unfortunate event.

The female announcer quickly made her way out onto the stage and approached the microphone as a mature woman that looked like she might be young woman's mother, rushed out onto the stage with a robe and helped her to stand up. She guided her towards the side door and put her arm around her shoulders as the young woman began to sob. The other contestants kept a mainly blank, straight face as she left the stage and faced directly in front of them as they ignored her departure seemingly unmoved. It was a very cold world the beauty pageant world, Genesis quickly decided as he actually realized that none of the young women had actually stood up and rushed out on the stage to assist the unfortunate young woman who had been humiliated by her outfit, stretched beyond its limits by the physical routine she'd inflicted upon it. It was competition, he thought and her humiliation eliminated one more competitor.

The final round arrived and the questions were posed by the judges as each woman stood in coordinated positions on small platforms positioned at various points along on the stage. The audience listened, smiled, nodded and clapped as they embraced the answers the models gave and the judges wrote things down silently. Five of the women on the stage were dismissed by the announcer as the judges eliminated them and they were asked to depart. The five women walked of the stage quietly, their eyes glazed over with what appeared to be tears waiting to be shed. Disappointment and hurt adorned each painful step they took as they walked off the platform subdued, rejected and despondent. Luckily Genevieve still remained on stage as the five women were then narrowed down to the final three and the judges prepared to announce the winners and runners up. Paula Perkins, Genevieve's arch rival, still however remained on the stage as one of the final three as Genesis heard her name being called out. Genesis began to worry slightly, he hoped that Genevieve and her mother had done enough to overcome the threat she posed and that Genevieve would ultimately be victorious.

"In third place we have Sylvia Montague." The female announcer stated as she beckoned towards a young woman, who walked towards her and handed her a large bunch of flowers and a small diamond tiara.

The very pretty young woman rushed towards her and accepted the flowers as she bowed her head and allowed the announcer to place the tiara upon it. She then stood on the smallest block on a small three block stage in front of the judges and smiled. Paula Perkins and Genevieve remained positioned on the main stage nearby as they waited for the next announcements. The announcer held an envelope in her hand that contained the name of the winner and final runner up and the audience fell totally silent as they waited and watched her every movement. Genesis held his breath as she held it up in the air and prepared to open it. A few seconds later it was all over as the announcer proclaimed the winner.

"Genevieve Mansfield you are the winner of the Annual Luscious Ladies Beauty Pageant." The announcer remarked. "Please come forward and accept your crown."

Music immediately started to play in the background, it was loud and triumphant as Genevieve approached the announcer and bent her head forward politely to accept her crown. Paula Perkins glanced at Genevieve with what appeared to be malice in her eyes as she observed the crowning of her arch rival. A few seconds later the female announcer beckoned towards Paula Perkins and announced her as the runner up as she placed a smaller tiara upon her head and handed her a slightly smaller bunch of flowers. The three young women then stood on the three step stage totally still their face painted with large smiles as the journalists around the room took photos of them. The female announcer hung sashes over the three young women's bodies and then thanked the judges for attending as the mothers of the three young women rushed out onto the stage and started to hug them proudly.

Once the crowd had dispersed from the room and the judges had left, Genevieve stepped down from the top step of the small stage and quickly walked towards where Genesis was seated. She smiled as she walked down the steps at the side of the stage and approached the seat he was still seated in. He'd decided to wait just to see Genevieve and her mother to congratulate them on their victory and had not yet deserted the banqueting hall.

Genesis smiled as Genevieve approached him. "This is such a huge achievement." Genesis encouraged as he smiled and nodded at her. "Well done."

"Thank you so much for all your help." Genevieve insisted appreciatively. "You really made a huge difference, the difference between winning and losing. I couldn't have done it without you."

"It's okay. It's my job, just like modelling is now your job." Genesis replied as he smiled at her.

Sandra approached them both and smiled. "Shall we go for dinner to celebrate?" She asked. "We could have some cocktails and perhaps even a little champagne. My treat."

Genesis smiled and then shook his head. "I couldn't possibly but thanks for inviting me. It's been very interesting and well done to you both. I have a dinner appointment that I have to attend." Genesis insisted.

"I understand." Sandra replied. "Thank you Genesis for helping us win. We've been trying for years. Paula Perkins just always seemed to have the edge over Genevieve. I was beginning to think we might have to travel to another country just to face other contestants. It's just been impossible for Genevieve to be placed first whenever Paula is present. The curse of Paula Perkins has now been broken and now my daughter has what she's worked so hard for. Thank you."

Genesis smiled as he glanced around the banqueting room once more which now was only occupied by a few contestants and their parents and nodded. "It's nothing, it's my job to help people. It's what I get paid for." He insisted humbly.

Sandra stretched out a hand towards him. "I doubt we'll see you again." Sandra said as she prepared to bid Genesis farewell. "We probably won't have much time for socializing now and Genevieve now has all the mind adaptations she needed."

Genesis nodded. "I understand. Genevieve I wish you the best of luck with your career and if you ever met a computer technician that you salsa dance with try not to let him down." Genesis remarked as he smiled.

The two women looked at each other slightly confused by his remark as Genesis walked away from them both and smiled. Genevieve, to him represented the next generation of Cherise's and one day perhaps, she too would hold a heart in her hands like Cherise had held his, hopefully though she'd be kinder and wouldn't actually crush it. Genesis had now had a glimpse into the world that Cherise had actually lived in and he now fully understood, how different that lifestyle was from his more humble, simple existence.

The next week, Genesis put beauty pageants behind him as he met with Titus once more as their regular appointments together continued. Titus had become his most regular client and at each appointment, he seemed to be hungrier and hungrier for a more exciting thrill every time they met. Money was no object it seemed as Titus lavished as much of his disposable income as he wanted to on the various mind adaptations offered by New Minds Inc. and explored each desire he wanted to see manifest in his life, personality and behavior.

"I've done the two woman thing, many times now Genesis. Now, I'd actually like to increase my personality levels again so I can actually participate in an orgy." Titus insisted as he sat opposite Genesis in his consultation room one afternoon.

"Have you done the mile high thing?" Genesis teased playfully as he tried to curb his appetite and calm his desires down slightly.

"More than done it. I was given oral sex in my private jet and in the business class toilets of a public commercial plane by beautiful strangers several times." Titus replied as he flashed a grin at Genesis. "I need something more now."

The response illustrated clearly to Genesis, that now Titus's desires were actually exceeding his capabilities to control them and he had absolutely no intention of slowing down or attempting to do so. Genesis quietly began to wonder if Titus would ever be truly satisfied by what he could offer him. He shrugged and nodded a few seconds later as he agreed to participate fully in his request and pander to his appetite. Caton's instructions had been absolutely clear, Genesis was simply give this man whatever he wanted and that was exactly what he was going to do. Moral and ethical deliberations were not his to hold and he was not in a position to actually restrict Titus's consumption.

"Jump on the couch and I'll see what I can do." Genesis replied as he smiled politely.

Not even a minute passed as Titus quickly made his way towards the couch willingly and leapt up onto it as he complied with Genesis's instructions enthusiastically. Genesis watched him for a moment as he contemplated as to whether he was actually ruining this man for life or simply giving a customer something extra he could actually handle. The reality was Titus's requests and actual mind adaptations far exceeded the usual desires and work he performed for the majority of his clients and the nature of his requests, Genesis knew, was delving deep into a pit of infinite desires that would grow and grow until perhaps one day they consumed him. Titus wanted to experience extreme pleasure and there might be no return from the depths of extreme lust he wanted to indulge in and that scared Genesis a little. The memories of his participation in his fantasies would be engraved in his mind forever and it was most likely he would never forget them. Those memories might even prompt Titus to seek out similar experiences time and time again and he may never actually be able to return to the innocence of life he'd once enjoyed.

Thoughts provoked Genesis's mind as he prepared to make the changes Titus had requested, perhaps Titus would never be able to actually ever marry and settle down in a relatively faithful marriage as he continued to venture further down this road. Would Titus ever be able to change himself and become more faithful and less adventurous or would he simply have to marry someone who was also more liberal and likeminded at the end of his exploration? Would his exploration ever actually end? The questions lay within his mind unanswered, for the time being the truth and answers were impossible to predict or foresee, with any kind of precision. Titus was on a rollercoaster of lust that explored the highest heights and lowest dips of sexual arousal and for now, he simply had no intention of getting of that ride. The questions and speculation blurred into irrelevance as Genesis pushed firmly through his own moral boundaries and common sense and simply succumbed fully to Titus's requests.

Caton's words from one of his initial briefings echoed in Genesis's mind as he started to prepare the mind adaptations required. "We're not here to judge people Genesis. Just to optimize their experiences of life whilst on this earth."

Inside himself, Genesis knew he was crossing a line within his own moral conscience but he pushed straight through it nonetheless. His job required him to be morally neutral and for the first time in his entire life, he was actually having to introspectively consider, that perhaps he was slightly more judgmental than even he, himself had actually realized. Titus waited for him as he prepared the system and instructed Adapt on the mind modifications that needed to be made. There was no going back now, for Titus or for Genesis.

The following week arrived and when Genesis met with Titus again for his follow up appointment, Genesis felt slightly relieved. Titus was ecstatic with the results of the last mind adaptations Genesis had performed and he expressed this overtly as Genesis listened.

"It's been truly great. I had the hottest sexual experience of my life." Titus insisted. "You should try these mind adaptations sometime."

Genesis smiled at his suggestion and pondered as to whether he actually should try to adapt his own mind for a moment as he glanced at Titus's face. His face seemed to shine with joy and although he'd never actually given much thought to such things or the possibilities that the Adapt system presented to him in reality, Genesis knew he'd never be able to attend an orgy, he'd be way to self-conscious and nervous. Sexual adventure was not something he'd delved into much throughout puberty or his young adulthood years, he'd enjoyed a few victories and had a few sexual relationships that had lasted beyond the rough fumbling's of teenage crushes but he'd never ventured into the dark areas of orgies, making love to multiple sexual partners at the same time or risky, public sexual liaisons. Was he a boring lover or a boring man, he was unsure, after all could one truly compare oneself to others, when such conclusions and opinions lay strictly in the minds of a third party.

The appointment with Titus soon ended as Genesis terminated the session, satisfied that Titus was pleased. Whether or not he would actually pursue Titus's suggestion and adapt his own mind was another matter entirely Genesis thought as gently pushed the thought to the back of his mind and escorted Titus to the reception area. It was something to think about perhaps at a later date.

The afternoon arrived as Genesis prepared enthusiastically to meet with Jade, who he had been actually looking forward to seeing for weeks. Unlike Titus, his sessions with Jade had been far less frequent and she'd actually let him know beforehand that today's appointment in all likelihood was likely to be her last. Genesis had scheduled her appointment that day as late as he possibly could, in his very last appointment slot so that he could spend a little more time with her if the opportunity actually presented itself.

"I'm finding the mind adaptations a little addictive." Jade had explained to him at her prior session as she'd attempted to justify her departure from Genesis's current client list. "The more I fine tune myself, the more I find, I'm dissatisfied with other things about myself."

The explanation she provided made total sense to Genesis, who had actually observed that a few of his clients become much more regular than they'd planned to be originally, once they'd experienced and enjoyed one or two mind adaptations they'd made more appointments and requested other adaptations. He contemplated quietly as he ate his lunch and prepared for the afternoon, whether he should actually increase his own confidence levels and reduce his levels of moral determination slightly as he yearned for Jade to arrive and her appointment to begin. Before Jade actually departed from his life, Genesis had an intense desire to actually taste the forbidden fruit she possessed or at least make an attempt to do so and he felt if he didn't try to satisfy that lust he'd spend the rest of his entire life regretting and kicking himself for not even trying. The desire he harbored deep down inside actually went against most of the principles he actually believed in and that he'd managed to adhere to very successfully up until that point in time, those principles were firmly rooted inside him and actually opposed the prospect of becoming romantically or sexually involved with a client. Since this would however be Jade's final appointment, that factor teased Genesis playfully as he toyed with the notion that technically after today, Jade would no longer actually be his client. He simply couldn't resist the temptation as he justified it in his mind, surrendered to his desires and caved into his lusts.

Once Genesis finished lunch, he quickly inserted a fast insert implant into his own body, which meant he could apply adaptations to his own mind within just a couple of hours. Such implants were usually kept for emergencies and for special urgent client intakes but Genesis had decided that this was an urgent client intake and in this instance, he was the special client. The afternoon progressed as Genesis waited for the implant to situate itself and prepared to adapt his own mind. Now he would deviate from the purity of the brain he was born with, now he would finally take the plunge and dive into the depths of possibilities an amended mind presented to him. Now he would understand and experience what his clients experienced each time they came to see him.

Later that afternoon, when Jade actually arrived on time as usual she was sensually dressed and as appealing as ever. Genesis rubbed his hands together in eager anticipation as he followed her from the reception towards the elevator. He watched her walk as her hips swung from side to side in front of him, somewhat hypnotized and mesmerized by each step she took.

"Have you cut your hair Genesis?" Jade asked curiously as they stood by the elevator and waited for the doors to open as she inspected his physical exterior and attempted to identify what had changed about him.

"Nope my hair's still the same." Genesis replied as he shook his head and smiled. Genesis led her into the lift and it started to move rapidly upwards as he attempted to answer her underlying question. "I'm just wearing a different aftershave, perhaps that's what you've noticed." He remarked as they stepped out into the hallway and walked towards his consultation room door.

The response seemed to partially satisfy Jade as she sniffed the air and smiled. They entered inside the door of his consultation room and whilst doing so she drew a little closer to him as the door swished shut behind them both. Genesis could feel the warmth of her breath against his skin as she passed him and could control himself any longer as the inner turmoil caused by her close proximity, consumed him. He simply couldn't contain the whirlpool of arousal he felt as it swirled inside his groin and he became erect instantly.

The moment had been conquered by his body and Genesis simply couldn't resist as surrendered to his lust for Jade and pulled her closer as he held her waist, gently but firmly. Jade allowed him to do so as he began to caress and touch her body and his heart leapt with joy. He started to undress her frantically as he slid his hands in-between her legs and massaged her breasts vigorously. Deep within, Genesis knew he'd actually waited for this moment for a while and now he actually had it, he was going to make the most of it. She moaned with pleasure at his touch as he quickly led her to the nearby couch and lifted her up onto it. A few seconds later, he climbed on top of her and pulled her shiny, black skirt up to her waist quickly and then entered inside. He penetrated her as deeply as he could as she moaned with pleasure.

"Genesis I want you to make love to me in every way you can." Jade whispered. "Don't hold back, do whatever you want to me."

Genesis's senses were invigorated by her words as he pushed inside her more deeply and more frantically as he lost control. Jade groaned passionately as Genesis delved in and out of the wetness inside her body and relished each second, hungrily. A few minutes later once it was over and they had both climaxed, they lay totally still as they panted and giggled like children in each other's arms. Genesis was pleased that he'd satisfied her as he relaxed for a few minutes and recuperated. Once he was sure that he was actually strong enough and that he had recovered sufficiently, he stood up and gently pulled her towards him as he entered inside her once more and started to make love to her passionately and vigorously. She surrendered her body fully to him as she moaned with pleasure. The two carried on making love for what seemed like hours as Genesis made love to her in every way he could all over his consultation room as many times as he could, before their session was actually due to finish. All too soon Jade's session was over as she quickly dressed up and prepared to leave.

"I'll miss you Genesis." Jade murmured as she touched his lips with her finger. She kissed him softly on the lips. "You're a great lover."

At that precise moment, Genesis knew that not only would Jade never be coming back but that he would never actually ever see her again. Whatever had just transpired between them, was an event that would simply never, ever be repeated. Genesis turned to face Jade as he gazed into her eyes pleadingly and attempted to reassure her that this did not have to be the end for them both. That this could be just the beginning. How could she crush a flower that had not even fully bloomed, how could she kill the spirit of a love that had not yet fully been realized, without first giving it a chance to live, a chance to exist and to be felt in each of their hearts.

"You don't have to miss me." Genesis murmured a little sadly. "I'll be right here you can come by anytime or I can take you out anywhere you like. You don't have to have any adaptations, you can just come here to see me."

"That can never be Genesis." Jade explained sadly as she shook her head gently. "I'm getting married next week to a Pastor. My parents introduced us and I have to do this. You see our church is in a little bit of financial trouble and the union will solve all our problems." She explained as she glanced into his eyes. "My parents embezzled some money Genesis and now I have to help them or they could be ruined forever. They've never asked me for anything before and they gave me the world, it's the least I can do for them." She continued as her gaze fell to the floor.

The explanation although it made some kind of sense, made no actual sense to Genesis who nodded in understanding as he accepted her loyalty to her parents sadly. The illogicality of the truth gripped him as he scolded fate internally, why would fate place such a beautiful woman in his life and his hands, only to grab her out of his reach as soon as he moved closer to her.

He'd actually changed his own mind for Jade, he'd wanted her and she had wanted him, why couldn't life be that simple, how could fate be so cruel? How could life inflict such a harsh separation upon them both, before they'd even experienced the joy of being together? There were no answers to his questions and his heart started to ache as he missed her presence, before she'd even actually left the room. He was deeply touched by Jade's sense of duty to those who loved her and it was not something he could even dare to question. Genesis knew he'd only just arrived in Jade's life on the plane of incidental meetings and her duty to her parents far exceeded her duty towards him, they had been there since the very beginning, since her birth and they had even created her. Why did her duty to her parents seem to exceed her duty towards her own happiness he questioned inside, again this was simply something, he knew he had no right to even ask. The intimacy they'd shared, didn't actually give him the right to do so. Jade wasn't answerable to him and she wasn't obligated to even have a relationship with him, simply because they'd been naked and intimate together once.

"Our lives are not always our own Genesis." Jade explained as she stood up and prepared to leave. "With great wealth at times, comes great responsibility and lots of duties." She smiled as she spoke her final words and prepared to depart.

Genesis watched her silently as she left, frozen to the spot as if his feet were actually glued to the floor. He watched her leave his life, just like he'd watched Cherise leave his life, powerless to stop her. Deep down inside he wished he could stop her, reassure her and convince her to be his but as his heart sank to the floor and rooted him tightly to the ground, he knew it was already too late. He kicked himself inside silently as he contemplated why on earth, he simply could not foresee when the women in his life were going to leave him and why he left it far too late to convince them to change their minds, before they actually committed to other people. The door of the room swished shut as she departed from his consultation room and his life, somehow the door itself seemed to represent the closing of a door inside his heart as he shook his head in disbelief. He'd now lost Jade forever, just like he'd lost Cherise forever he concluded as a flurry of thoughts pulled away at his mind and he tried to find an answer to the question of why he kept failing the women in his life and himself. Why couldn't he convince them to stay, was he cursed in the arena of love, was it his destiny to be so close to finding a perfect life partner, just to have his heart broken and smashed to pieces on the floor time and time again? The question taunted him and no answers presented themselves within his mind as he glanced around the consultation room as his eyes searched every corner and inch but it lay still and empty before him much like his love life as it refused to provide any answers to him.

The reality was Genesis had even adapted his own mind for Jade but as he'd accepted her departure from the runway of his life as she'd left on a plane of refusal, that would quite simply never return to his destination, he now realized he'd implemented the changes way too late for them to actually have any real impact at all. The window of opportunity had closed and Jade's smile that sparkled like a sunrise was quite simply not one he would ever have the privilege to enjoy again, not in any kind of close proximity anyway. Genesis now felt like a failure as he analyzed the fact, that two of the women he'd most desired had simply walked straight out of his life and would never return, they'd slipped through his fingers like icy, cold water drops that had left his hands shivering, blanketed by the cold, icy loneliness of rejection.

The next few weeks for Genesis were dismal as he accepted Jade's departure and grieved for what he'd never had the chance to enjoy or really miss. It felt slightly strange to miss something or someone that had never actually been part of his life in a proper relationship but that was a mourning experience in itself. He mourned the very fact that he'd been robbed of the opportunity to try and have a relationship with Jade and that he'd not even been given a chance to do so and he was quieter than usual and more distant as he deliberated over the events with Jade and Cherise. Unusually not even Titus and his sexually adventurous shenanigans could cheer him up when his next appointment arrived.

Since that awful evening when Cherise had dumped Genesis, he'd deliberately stayed away from women for a while and kept his distance and Jade had actually been his first romantic encounter since his heart break on that dismal, horrible, devastating night.

Jade had somehow managed to reopen the door in his heart that he'd closed firmly after Cherise had left, she'd stolen his feelings for her as if by stealth as he'd fallen for her softly without even actually noticing it. The depths of his desires and his fondness for her had somehow grown and had flowed through his heart until it became a deep stream. It was only when Jade had actually stood up to leave that he'd actually realized how much he'd truly fallen for her, just she was actually departing. He'd definitely fallen for her and fallen flat on his face as she'd walked away and there had been no other loving pair of arms there to catch him.

The void and heartache that Cherise had caused when she'd departed had been appeased when he'd been rescued by his new job, which he'd utilized as a distraction as he'd channeled his efforts and attention into it. He'd come very close to falling into an abyss of a deep depression that he'd been very unsure he'd have been able to climb back out of, when it actually happened but as time had passed, his wounds had started to heal slowly as the medication that each day and night brought, soothed his crushed, weary, beaten spirit and reenergized him. Each night seemed to be almost like a silent, invisible nurse that collected a grain of hurt each day and carried it away. Time couldn't change the wounds but it faithfully reduced the hurt felt every day and made life a little more bearable to face.

Now, today, however those almost closed wounds, had been ripped back open as the despair and hurt started to seep out of the pores in Genesis's skin and cover every ounce of his flesh. He'd work harder, longer hours, Genesis thought, hard work had salvaged him from the trash heap he'd been dumped on by Cherise during his last heartbreak, hard work would help him now. It was the only solution and means of escape to avoid the painful, hurtful events that reality seemed to enjoy inflicting on him time and time again, through any woman he became romantically attached to.

LATTITUDE OR LONGITUDE

Over the next few weeks Genesis true to his decision, threw himself into work aggressively as he booked additional clients, worked longer hours and even worked some weekends. He met with Titus a couple of times as he attended some follow up sessions and the joy and happiness Titus expressed convinced Genesis that he'd been right to ignore his own moral judgments with regards to his situation. He'd definitely made the right decision as Titus seemed to be a very happy man.

The new clients Genesis was assigned to he approached with enthusiasm and vigor as he distracted himself with as much work as he possibly could and threw himself into other people's problems, in order to bury his own. The rejection he'd felt was pushed towards the back of his mind, where all the rest of his unwanted, painful memories kept each other company, a place where they actually lay dormant and ignored until a new painful reminder resuscitated them and they raised their ugly heads once more. It was completely impossible to bury the past Genesis quickly discovered and the most he could actually do was attempt to avoid it. Next time he decided, he'd be more careful and next time he would not allow himself to trip or fall in love with someone who didn't actually want him.

Several of the new clients Genesis had been assigned too, were more mature male clients and that relaxed him slightly as it meant there was absolutely no chance of any kind of romantic attraction. Genesis was strictly heterosexual and had never felt any kind of attraction towards a man which meant, his heart now was pretty safe at work as his male client intake increased. One of his new clients Victor puzzled him slightly however when they met. Victor was a mature man, fifty eight years old however he was actually involved with a much younger girlfriend, a woman in her late twenties. The coupling amused and confused Genesis somewhat as he attended sessions with Victor and listened to his elaborations over his demanding lover and the physical love life that he was struggling to provide her with. Although Victor was a mature man in terms of physical years, he actually looked much younger than his age. His handsome face and stylish presentation was very debonair and Genesis could appreciate why Victor might attract the attention of a much younger woman. Not only was Victor relatively good looking, stylish, a snappy dresser and in quite good shape, he was also extremely rich, having accumulated a mass of wealth in his younger years as a film star and he was used to being accompanied wherever he went, by very beautiful, younger women that he lavished with gifts and money. Although Victor had actually matured in age and started to settle down into more serious, longer lasting relationships, his taste in women had not actually matured with him and the younger women he'd lusted after in his youth, continued to capture his attention.

"I just love beautiful, younger women." Victor had explained to Genesis at their first appointment as he'd attempted to justify his position. "I make no excuses for that. I'm perfectly happy with the life I led and have lived."

Genesis had listened as he admired his honesty and frankness.

"I do however want to be a little bit more energetic, especially in the bedroom." Victor had explained. "Slightly better at seducing women and much more charming. I make no apologies for who I am and even though the women I see may be involved with other men, around their own age, I actually don't mind that at all. I can live with that. What I can't live with is a dreary life that I don't actually enjoy." He'd explained as he sought to clarify his personal philosophies towards life and romance.

The masked truths of the unspoken words that lay behind Victor's justifications had very quickly became apparent to Genesis as he'd listened to him elaborate further regarding his relationships with the opposite sex. He'd quite obviously been a bit of a playboy in his youth and squandered money on beautiful women, lived a fast lifestyle, filled with luxury and enjoyed his years, now however it seemed he had become very much aware that the women he'd romanced had simply been with him for as long as it worked in their favor and for whatever they could get out of him. Victor had absolutely failed on every level to build a deeper more meaningful relationship or connection with a woman he'd been romantically involved with and had simply continued reliving his youth over and over again and no woman he'd met had actually cared enough about him to be patient enough to insist he did so. Perhaps they had cared, Genesis thought as he prepared for his second consultation with Victor, perhaps he had driven them away with unfaithful and frivolous behavior that they simply could not accept or live with.

The second consultation with Victor was simple and straightforward as Genesis met him, indulged in his requests and provided him with exactly what he wanted. The moral issue of the younger female partner, Victor was romantically involved Genesis simply ignored as he adapted his personality without any hesitation at all. Genesis simply gave Victor, the life he wanted to enjoy and the life he actually wanted to live just as Caton had instructed him to.

The weeks passed as Genesis carried on with his usual routine, he worked throughout the week with clients and on system modifications and on the weekends he visited his parents a few times and did his best to avoid his mother's relationship questions. She wanted to know when he might start dating someone new and she was pushing him to actually do so. In some respects where he might have waited a while after a relationship ended to see if things would work out once more, when it came to Cherise, he actually didn't feel the obligation to do so. Cherise had moved on before she'd even dumped him and that meant he owed her no such loyalty or commitment. Quite often when Genesis left work very late in the evening, darkness had already coated the world and he would drive home quietly along the dark, city streets as he contemplated what the future might hold.

Late one evening as he went about his daily affairs and arrived home from work, he noticed a strange man lurking outside in the street near his home. The presence of the man aroused his suspicions slightly as he felt for some reason, he'd seen him before somewhere but couldn't place his face. Around the same time, strange things began to happen at work as the Adapt system seemed to start malfunctioning. Genesis and Raccoon often found themselves working throughout the weekends and late in the evenings during weekdays as they attempted to repair whatever damage had occurred. Caton held more frequent briefings with them as they tried to uncover what the root cause actually was. Monday mornings were now filled with briefings about system problems as the problems increased and caused more and more interruptions to the daily operations of New Minds Inc. Whatever the problem was, it was not simply going to go away.

"Do we have a virus?" Caton asked Raccoon and Genesis politely as he paced his office in front of them one Monday morning and questioned them both after a system failure the previous Friday afternoon.

"Not that I can see." Raccoon replied. "I've interrogated the system fully and I haven't been able to find anything that would indicate a malicious attack of that kind."

"Keep working on it and let me know when you can actually establish what is going on." Caton replied anxiously as he rubbed his chin.

"We've had more than three disruptions now and these problems are starting to have an impact on our clients."

The briefing ended as Raccoon and Genesis left his office with glum expressions on their faces. Their failure to locate the source of the problem, address it and resolve it, was like a kick in the face. Throughout the briefing, they'd felt Caton's disappointment pierce through their skin as his eyes had stared at their faces and demanded an answer. There was however no answer to be found, not yet anyway and the two men quite simply had no idea what was going on or who was responsible for causing it. The search of the system began to consume every spare moment they had as they worked late most evenings and through some weekends. Genesis began to become frustrated as the source of their bone of discontent evaded them illusively.

"Do you think it's a design flaw inside the system architecture itself?" Genesis asked Raccoon late one evening as they abandoned the search and surrendered to fatigue as the prepared to go home.

"Nope, the Adapt system is perfect and was perfect." Raccoon explained. "We haven't had a problem ever and I've been here since Caton actually started the business." He remarked as they walked through the reception area.

They nodded to acknowledge the night security guard who was by now seated firmly behind the reception desk, Gemma the receptionist had abandoned her post and gone home several hours beforehand, unlike them. The security guard, a stout man with a gristly beard was in his late fifties. He didn't seem surprised to see them leave late as the pair had left late frequently over the past few weeks and he'd become somewhat used to their departure throughout his shift. He simply nodded his head at them and then unlocked the front door as he touched the screen in front of him and it swung open as he allowed them to exit. A man of few words who seemed to embrace the night and the solitude it provided, he rarely even met any employees that belonged to the company who's assets he guarded each night, let alone ever speak to them. The two men left quietly as they deserted their conversation, it was inappropriate to continue such a discussion in his presence, they quickly concluded as they fell silent. Although the security guard was actually an employee just as they were, the sensitive nature of what they were investigating demanded a confidential approach, something both men were acutely aware off. They didn't discuss these matters in front of anyone beside themselves and Caton. Once in the parking lot they headed towards their cars defeated and exhausted, whatever was wrong with the Adapt system for now the solution remained firmly outside their grasp and staying at work even later that evening simply wouldn't resolve that.

Throughout the next few weeks Genesis arrived home late at night quite often and on several occasions as he exited his car, he felt as if he was definitely being watched by someone as he walked towards his front door. Who was doing the actual watching and how often they were actually doing it however, he couldn't actually be certain. The discomfort Genesis felt as a result was as if a spider had crawled onto his body and was crawling all over his skin however each time he searched for the source of discomfort, the spider of discomfort seemed to simply hide away in the layers of his clothes invisible to the naked eye.

The feeling niggled and gnawed away at him and he simply couldn't trace it's source, shake it off or eliminate it. Genesis yearned to discuss the strange man's presence outside his home with Caton or Raccoon, but resisted the urge to do so through fear. The two men may ridicule him, Genesis decided and there was no actual proof that anyone was actually following him at all and even less proof that this might possibly be connected to New Minds Inc. or the system problems the company was actually experiencing. Genesis kept his words, tightly behind his lips and buried the thoughts deep within his mind as he imprisoned them indefinitely.

The disruptions to the system continued to happen and became more frequent as both Raccoon and Genesis strived to resolve the issues and trace the source, however it was like fighting a blazing fire with a drizzle of water, no sooner had one spot been extinguished and one problem resolved, another one would simply spiral out of control and take its place. Despite the problems, they managed to keep the disruption to clients at a minimum as appointments scheduled later in the afternoon towards the evening were abandoned by consultants and weekend appointments were avoided completely. By rescheduling most of the client appointments to the usual hours of the working week, it allowed Genesis and Raccoon to control the system throughout the day and work on it freely on the weekends and evenings, when there were no clients around.

A collective employee briefing was held and Caton requested everyone's attendance, except for the chefs and security staff. He paced the room as he glanced nervously at the audience of employees in front of him as they watched him. Caton prided himself on his leadership, his ability to find solutions and despite his proactive approach somehow he'd now found himself drowning in inability, negativity and defeat. He contemplated for a few moments as he remained silent as to how he could actually reassure a room full of people that the situation was under control, when he actually knew in reality, he had no real answers at all to provide to them.

The boardroom where the meeting was being held was situated very close to the reception area and the room was full, everyone had abandoned their consultation rooms and rescheduled their meetings with clients that morning on the previous Friday afternoon at Caton's request. There were some faces in attendance that Genesis rarely saw, like the other six consultants that were situated on the floors above him and a female face that he'd never actually ever seen at all, the woman the foreign face belonged to, it later transpired was an external security advisor. Her name was Felicity. The security advisor stood at the front of the room with Caton as the consultants sat around the huge, black, glossy meeting table in front of them quietly as they waited for Caton to speak. Felicity was in her late forties and had jet black hair, dark brown eyes and was what Genesis would describe as more handsome than beautiful in that she had a strong jaw line that seemed almost as if it had been chiseled to perfection by a carpenter.

"We seem to have a little bit of problem on our hands." Caton started to explain as he faced the expectant employees and mustered up some grains of courage inside him. "This is Felicity Rankin, a very private, security specialist I've known for years. She's come on board to assist us and help manage this crisis we seem to be facing." Caton explained calmly as he avoided direct eye contact with everyone seated directly in front of him, fearful that he may betray the confident, calm image he was attempting to present. "No one must breathe a word regarding these issues to anyone external to the company. We are vulnerable right now and that would make us candidates for hostile takeover bids if the word actually got out." He insisted. "That includes partners, wives, husbands, boyfriends and so on. Your love and dedication to them does not justify a breach of confidentiality or the divulgence of my company's confidential, delicate condition under any circumstances."

The consultants in the room nodded obediently as they listened to Caton speak and accepted his instructions, their loyalty to him wasn't a hard ask and he knew it. Caton paid them extremely well and for that additional luxury, there were additional expectations and confidentiality was quite simply one of those expectations that was nonnegotiable. The room full of nodding heads appeased Caton as he carried on with the briefing.

Genesis sat and listened as he began to speculate whether or not he should actually mention his concerns to Caton once more regarding the man he'd seen late at night outside his home. Perhaps he could even mention it to the external security expert he thought, they may be more likely to accept his suspicions. The meeting concluded an hour or so later as all the consultants made their way out of the room and returned to their consultation rooms, slightly distracted by the gloomy nature of the event. Usually when Caton called or held a briefing, it was to celebrate a positive event such as the awarding of salary bonuses, extra staff recreational activities or some other kind of perk that he'd actually arranged. This briefing had been a far cry from what they were used to and the glum expression on their faces reflected that.

"We may have to take on less new clients and see existing clients more sparsely until this situation is resolved." Caton had explained throughout the briefing. "This will have an impact on your bonuses, but there is very little I can do about it for now."

The bonus scheme Caton had implemented, meant that for each client who attended ten sessions or more, a consultant would receive a special bonus sum that was usually a five percent increase on top of that particular month's salary. Whilst the figure was not particularly significant to the consultants who were paid well enough, at the end of each year the consultant who had accumulated the most bonuses throughout the year would be given five days extra holiday. Holidays were treasured by the staff due to the often long and unsocial working hours and that was the main reason for the glum mood as the small board room emptied and Caton and Felicity were left alone.

"Are there any new employees?" Felicity enquired politely as she closed the meeting room door and faced Caton. "You know how it is Caton, usually these things are an inside job and quite often the perpetrator finds a weakness within the company to infiltrate. That weakness is usually one of your staff."

The look on Caton's face was one of horror as he contemplated the possibility for a moment that perhaps one of his own trusted employees might be actually responsible for the misfortune and devastating events that had transpired.

"Come on they wouldn't Felicity." He returned as he defended the people he had trusted in and employed. "I pay them a lot. They enjoy working here."

"Don't be naive Caton a saboteur may even pay them more than you do. They might be stealing secrets, sabotaging your company and causing mayhem for a larger sum than they're monthly pay-packet." Felicity replied as she shook her head at Caton.

Caton they both knew was an idealist in that he simply believed that if you did right by the world and the people within it that would be reciprocated and they would simply do right by you. It was his main weakness and Felicity had realized that many years ago.

"Okay, okay we have one new employee." Caton replied as he raised his hands in the air and surrendered to her request. "He started a while ago but he's the most recent. His name is Genesis."

"Good, I'll put him under twenty four hour surveillance immediately and let you know if anything comes up." Felicity confirmed as she nodded her head. "Anyone else I should pay a little more attention to? Just whilst I'm there, I mean if I'm doing one, it won't take much more effort to do a few more. Who has the most access to the core system?"

"Raccoon. He's our main developer and engineer." Caton answered as he shook his head. "It definitely wouldn't be anything to do with him, he's been here since the New Minds Inc. opened."

"People change Caton. Are you the same as when you were three years old?" Felicity questioned.

"There is a deep philosophical theory that states the first few years of our lives are actually our formative years, so I'm probably actually, technically not really that different." Caton replied as he attempted to challenge her consideration of Raccoon as a suspect.

"I'll watch him too." Felicity concluded. "Any huge spenders amongst your staff? People who love the lavish luxuries in life just a little bit too much?"

Caton hesitated for a moment as he considered a few consultants names inside his mind and then shook his head quickly.

"Come on Caton, there has to be at least one." Felicity insisted. "This is not going to work if you're not going to be honest with me."

Felicity, Caton knew was very good at her job and her sharp perceptive instincts had caught him attempting to protect those he employed from her scrutiny. He knew he had to surrender someone or she'd never let the matter rest. "Okay, okay. There's one." He admitted as he succumbed to Felicity's determined approach and faced her, her eyes were laced with accusations as she seemed to search his inner soul to extract the truth. "Edgar seems to spend a lot, however I've always assumed most of this expenditure is debt financed, though I've never actually bothered to check."

"Great now we have three and we started ten minutes ago with none." Felicity said as a smile of satisfaction grew on her face.

"It might actually be none of them though, so you could be wrong Felicity." Caton insisted. "That is possible."

Felicity laughed at his optimism.

The two left the room as Caton escorted Felicity out of the building and they headed towards her car as they walked they scheduled their next meeting. The parking lot was empty as they approached the large, silver saloon she drove.

Felicity stood by the door of her car as she smiled at Caton. "I hope I'm wrong Caton." Felicity insisted. "Sincerely I do. I'd love nothing more than for your trust in human beings and your employees to actually be validated."

A few minutes later as the silver car drove off into the distance, Caton stood and watched it disappear as he shook his head thoughtfully. The employees he'd employed he absolutely trusted, but he also trusted Felicity and that trust ran even more deeply through his veins. Caton could quite comfortably entrust Felicity with any of the strands of hair that sat on the head of his life as he knew she would quite simply, never, ever betray him. Her judgment, loyalty and protection of Caton over the years had been anchored in depths of sincerity, truthfulness and dignity that were unfathomable, no human being had ever been as honest to him in his entire life, than Felicity had. Those who came into contact with Caton usually guarded their words in awe of and intimidated by his intellect, his position and his wealth, through fear they may offend or upset him. Sometimes other people attempted to lie to him to take advantage of his soft nature, but Felicity absolutely never lied to him, she was as blunt as a piece of sandpaper and there was no subtlety, politeness or tact in her being that forced her to evade the truth, she quite simply told you the truth, whether you actually wanted to hear it or not.

Throughout the next few weeks Genesis observed the results of his work at New Minds Inc. as a variety of clients came and went. Many of them related stories to him of how much they were enjoying life since they'd undergone the adaptations he'd performed in their minds and the impact they had on their lives was predominantly positive. A deeper desire however grew inside him as he felt provoked to enjoy his own life more and craved a deeper connection to other human beings. Single life, many people would debate and argue, could be interesting and fulfilling but for Genesis he simply didn't agree with those philosophies. He loved to have a partner, he loved being in love and loved the enjoyment that accompanied that experience. Singleness to him was a crucifix that represented the burden of carrying an empty life that had been sapped of all the lifeblood it required, like a brown, withered leave that lay on the ground waiting as nature, insects and time decayed, decomposed and eradicated it until it was actually nothing.

The temptation to adapt his own mind once more was growing as he sought to live his life again more fully and decorate the walls of his life with a woman's presence. He needed to be less sensitive and more adventurous, he decided and definitely less monogamous. Perhaps, he thought by seeing more than one woman at a time, he could reduce the level of risk and his exposure to potential heartbreak through partner diversification. Titus and his investment theories had started to rub off on him.

The consultation room he usually occupied with clients was empty as he contemplated more deeply a potential remedy to his loneliness, the particles of darkness from the evening's presence filled the air around him and rested delicately on top of him like a blanket of snow as he sat alone and simply thought about his own life. There were no rules as far as he was aware when it actually came to employees adapting their own minds and he had already somewhat indulged in doing so, albeit relatively mildly. Caton hadn't expressed any such rules to him at any of their briefings and had simply left him to decide for himself whether or not he wished to sample the delicacies the Adapt system had to offer.

The system problems had continued to hamper the company and although they hadn't seemed to get any worse since Felicity had arrived, as a result his client list was slightly less busy. Genesis now found he actually spent more hours working with Raccoon as they analyzed the system and attempted to find the cause, which meant instead of actually working less hours, he was actually working more. Sometimes he still felt the feeling of being followed home at night but since he'd seen no sign or indication that he actually was, he'd simply chalked the strange man he'd seen in the street outside his home down to coincidence.

He touched the screen in front of him and it filled with an image of his brain as he prepared to access his own mind map and make further adaptations to his own mind. He knew exactly what he wanted to do as he quickly increased his levels of confidence and sensuality and then reduced his levels of fear and loyalty. A few seconds later he jumped onto the couch nearby that was usually occupied by his clients and pulled the capsule lid over his head as he prepared for his mind makeover. This time Genesis was pushing the personality points of his brain map nearer to the extreme as he'd maneuvered them from their current position and changed the points of longitude and latitude they currently sat upon. He'd initialized changes that were vastly different from his current status within the various components of his mind and personality but right now he cared very little for the overall impact those changes would actually have upon his life, in the longer term. Genesis needed something his empty, void life wasn't currently providing and that something the mind adaptations would actually provide.

Thirty minutes later when Genesis left the building he ignored the usual roads that led to his home and instead headed straight towards the city center and a hotel with a bar. Hotel bars he'd determined earlier that day were the best place to pick up women, they were unlike a typical bar in that they were slightly more intimate and had the added bonus that they actually provided a room facility nearby that he could easily utilize to satisfy his sexual desires, if the opportunity arose. This meant Genesis could actually avoid having to face the intimacy and inconvenience of bringing a woman he didn't know back to his home. Although his home wasn't much to write home about, it was still very much his own personal space and he felt slightly uncomfortable about bringing unknown, random women there for a night of passion as the only woman who had visited it throughout the past year had actually been Cherise.

The first hotel bar he entered inside was a middle of the range, three star hotel and the foyer was quite empty as he made his way towards the bar. The bar itself was quite busy and he stepped inside the glass doors, ordered a whisky and then sat down on an unoccupied bar stool as he watched the other occupants of the bar mill around him quietly. None of the women inside the bar, that appeared to be alone appealed to him much however and he quickly finished his drink and departed. He'd try another bar.

The next hotel bar he visited which was around a block or so away looked slightly more promising as he entered inside and immediately found a few more attractive females seated by the bar on their own. One was very slim, with golden, blonde hair that cascaded down over her shoulders from a tall, elaborate hair style she'd managed to create. Perhaps she'd been to the hair salon that day, he thought.

Another woman seated along the row of bar stools, had olive skin and dark, striking locks that sat gently upon on her neck, she was also very pretty. A third woman however sparked his interest somewhat more as he explored all the females within the bar that seemed to be alone and sized them up according to his physical preferences. The final woman he noticed was not actually as facially pretty as the other two women but she had an amazing cleavage, which was clearly on display. He licked his lips as he glanced at her body and noticed that her wide hips and thick thighs were partly exposed, her pert butt seemed to stand to attention as she stood up for a moment and ordered another drink from the server behind the bar. His mouth started to salivate as waves of lust welled up inside him and surged through his body like an electric pulse.

Deep inside him the sexual desire he felt seemed to almost overpower him as it drove him towards the other end of the bar where the third female was actually seated and he quickly sat down on an empty bar stool next to her. He quickly offered to pay for the drink she'd just ordered and the attractive woman in her mid-thirties agreed as she turned to face him and smiled appreciatively. Conversation between them flowed almost as quickly as the alcohol they consumed as they started to engage in small talk and Genesis quickly discovered that her name was Tiffany. Not long afterwards, much to Genesis's delight she actually accepted his invitation to retreat to a hotel room within the hotel they were actually situated inside as he basked in warmth of acceptance that Tiffany had provided. She'd embraced his suggestion very easily. The two exited the bar and walked into the reception area as Genesis prepared to book a room.

"I'll just be a minute. Let me get my room keycard." Genesis insisted as Tiffany waited by the doorway that led to the elevators nearby on the edge of the foyer.

He quickly rushed over towards the reception desk, booked and paid for a room as he smiled at the receptionist who handed him the room key card.

"Your room is on the first floor." The male receptionist remarked as he smiled. "Just turn left when you exit the elevator."

The directions he provided were appreciated as Genesis returned quickly to Tiffany's side. Hunting for a hotel room right now that he was actually already supposed to be staying would not be a good look or a desirable eventuality and the receptionist had spared him that possible embarrassment and he was essentially very relieved. Such a search Genesis knew would send a clear message to Tiffany that he was not actually a guest at the hotel and may reveal the slightly more calculated, seedy nature of his visit there. The motivations behind his visit to the hotel, Genesis was aware were not entirely elegant and he had absolutely no desire to reveal the seedy nature of that truth to anyone, let alone a woman he was attempting to sleep with. She wouldn't be impressed.

Once Genesis returned to Tiffany's side he smiled at her enthusiastically as he held the keycard up in the air and nodded at her confidently. He took her arm gently and led her towards the elevator that was already waiting for them, open and expectant as it waited to receive more guests and transport them to the relevant floor. The two stepped inside and smiled at each other. Whilst Genesis was polite and seemed to display some affection towards Tiffany, he actually knew inside he had absolutely no intentions of ever actually seeing her again. This liaison was purely going to be a sexual, animalistic, night of passion which may never actually be repeated and the raw nature of Genesis's intentions, meant that he'd skipped through some of the usual dating formalities he participated in with women he was romantically interested in. Genesis didn't even actually bother to ask if Tiffany was married and as they exited the elevator Genesis quickly realized, he actually didn't care even if she was.

When the two arrived outside the hotel room that Genesis had booked, they both entered inside and he quickly made his way towards the small, black, fridge bar, situated at one side of the room. He opened the small door and quickly took a bottle of chilled wine. Tiffany didn't actually ask him if he was married either and as he handed her a glass of wine and they sat down on a large, gold, duvet that adorned a huge king-size bed, he felt relieved that she hadn't.   Tiffany it seemed fully understood why they were both there and no questions meant there was no concern about any kind of possible relationship between them.   For a few minutes the two sat on the bed as they sipped wine from their glasses in silence.   There was an appreciation between them, that seemed to remain unspoken as they enjoyed simply being a man and woman that were sexually attracted to each other and about to engage in exploring that attraction.

"I don't usually do this kind of thing." Tiffany explained as she broke the silence between them and giggled.   "You know, meet guys in a bar and go back to their rooms."   She volunteered the remarks as she suddenly began to feel a little self-conscious about her presence in the hotel room as she sought to justify her presence to not only Genesis, but also herself.

Genesis immediately became aware that Tiffany was starting to feel a little uncomfortable and attempting to rationalize their interaction as he quickly sought to appease her mind and took the glass from her hand and put it down on the dressing table nearby. He faced her as he knelt down in front of her, his hands empty and ready to embrace her body and then a few seconds later, he leant forward and kissed her lips passionately as he slipped his hands into the top of her dress and started to massage her breasts gently. Invigorated and excited by the passion he felt stir deep inside him that flurried around his body like a snowstorm, he then started to explore her body in a more vigorous manner with his lips and hands. Genesis pushed her backwards and she fell gently down onto the bed as he pulled up her dress and quickly slipped his hand in-between her legs.

The wetness inside her that greeted him, excited him further as he quickly removed his trousers and shirt and penetrated her eagerly. He pushed himself deep inside her as she groaned. A few seconds later, he lifted her up and pushed her up against a wall nearby and entered her from behind as she gasped. The mood within him was frantic as he began to pound her body vigorously and she moaned with delight. It was over in minutes however as Genesis reached his peak and climaxed, unable to control his excitement. He kissed her neck passionately as he extracted himself from her body and then quickly led her towards the adjoining bathroom nearby.

"I want to make love to you all night." He explained in a husky tone. "Your body was made for love making and for me to make love to you."

Tiffany giggled as she followed him into the bathroom nearby and dropped her black, lycra dress, bra and matching thongs onto the floor of the hotel room as they walked. Genesis pulled her gently into the shower and turned on the taps as water started to cascade down onto their naked bodies.

The shower water was warm, refreshing and crisp as it started to beat down against their flesh. They washed each other playfully for a few minutes before Genesis kissed Tiffany passionately to indicate that he was ready to delve inside her once more. Tiffany giggled again. Once more Genesis placed his hands on her breasts and caressed them, he then placed his hand on her shoulders and started to push her gently down towards the ground onto her knees as the water continued to cascade over them both and embrace their bodies. Tiffany obliged and complied with his desires as she started to caress his chest with her mouth and tease his navel with her tongue. She lowered her body closer to the floor as she knelt down on her knees in front of him. Genesis groaned with pleasure as she teased him playfully with her lips and tongue and prolonged the urge he desired to be fulfilled.

A few seconds later as she accepted him into her wet mouth and began to orally pleasure him, Genesis held her head as he pushed himself deeper inside her. He began to pound her mouth vigorously, unable to hold himself back any longer as the pleasure surged through his body with an intensity he hadn't experienced for a very long time. Genesis needed this. He needed her body. Tiffany could have just been any woman that he'd actually stumbled upon that night and simply represented a female body that he'd required to fulfill the lust and tension building inside of him, desires that he could quite simply, no longer control. Like an animal almost he continued to pound away deeper and harder as she gripped his round buttocks with her hands and he groaned with intense pleasure.

That night had opened a door to enjoyment that almost overwhelmed Genesis as he participated in the pleasures it offered, throughout his entire relationship with Cherise he'd never once felt as sexually free as he felt right now. Genesis had often sought to control himself when he was around Cherise, even in the bedroom desperate not to offend her. Now, however with this stranger Genesis felt a strange sense of sexual liberation and it was almost intoxicating. Now he could actually enjoy the things he longed to do free from the inhibitions of a woman who may judge him negatively. Now he was free from the thought that his actions in the bedroom, may actually have an impact on the future of his long term relationship. The sexual arousal he felt was intense as it consumed his body and mind as he climaxed again. Pleasure gripped every inch of his body in an almost paralyzing clinch as he surrendered to it fully and ejaculated.

A few minutes later Genesis gently took Tiffany's arm as he raised her up to her feet and then began to gently wash her. He whispered softly into her ear. "Now I'm going to make you scream with pleasure." He insisted. "I'll make you feel like no other man has ever made you feel." He murmured as he turned her towards him and caressed her neck and chest greedily with his hands and lips.

The water stopped falling as Genesis turned it off and then led Tiffany back to the bedroom once more. He lay her down on the bed and then entered inside her a little more gently. Passion soon overtook him however as he delved deeper inside her and his body moved faster and faster as she groaned with enjoyment and gripped onto his back with her hands. His thrusts became more frantic as he sought to bring her to a point of climax and pounded into her body as she screamed with delight. A few minutes later as Tiffany climaxed Genesis sighed with relief as he quickly released himself and climaxed also. He'd finally satisfied her.

The next morning when Genesis attended work as usual, tired but pleased about the previous night which he'd enjoyed immensely, he contemplated how he would spend the next weekend. The hotel bar had worked out wonderfully for him and he decided to seek out a few more similar bars in the heart of the city and occupy his weekend with any sexual encounters he could find there. He'd found a new outlet and recreational activity to fill the dull hours of his free time, one that allowed him to fully participate in intimacy without the complex, emotional entanglements of a messy relationship and now, he was determined to make the most of his discovery.

The Monday morning was quiet as Caton met with Felicity and they discussed the investigation further. She'd organized surveillance of the three employees, she'd felt had greater access or deeper motives and those she'd felt may actually inflict harm onto Caton's work and business. Raccoon, Genesis and Edgar had been followed as a result, watched and monitored but all three men remained totally oblivious to Felicity's intrusion. Caton urged Felicity to either prove that she had a reason to keep them under surveillance or to cease the operation as they met that Monday morning.

"Found anything yet?" Caton enquired as they sat in his office.

"Not yet." Felicity replied as she shook her head.

"See I told you, it's not any of those guys." Caton remarked as he challenged her instincts. "I'm quite careful about employees. I just don't employ anyone I don't feel right about."

"Look Caton until we're sure, everyone is a suspect." Felicity replied. "Everyone has their instincts but sometimes even our instincts are wrong, we're only human."

"I think it's a corporate thing. A competitor perhaps trying to sabotage the system and steal the intellectual property it was built on." Caton explained.

"Yes but what better way to do that, than through an employee, someone you trust, someone you've given access too." Felicity ventured. "I'll keep watching him for another few weeks and if I don't get anything on any of them I'll stop." She promised.

Caton nodded.

The room fell silent as Caton reflected internally for a moment thoughtfully as he contemplated who could possibly be attacking his company and why. Perhaps it was the system itself he thought, perhaps Adapt had evolved and was creating these malfunctions in some kind of act of rebellion. Or perhaps it was one of the original four scientists that he'd initially built the system with, perhaps they wanted more money that the sums he'd paid them for the development work they'd done. There were other possibilities.

"What if we're totally on the wrong track." Caton suggested as he stood up paced his office as he glanced at Felicity. "I mean there are other people who could be trying to sabotage the system or it could be an internal system thing and nothing to actually do with anyone else at all."

His remark pleased Felicity who jumped up to her feet as she accepted the possibility that there might be other suspects she could sink her teeth into. The three she was watching so far had rendered little in terms of real results and she was anxious to actually deliver something. She loathed not being successful in any investigation she undertook and a lack of results indicated a failure on her part as it undermined her competence. Whatever suggestions Caton might have right now, she was more than willing to explore and investigate further as she encouraged him.

"Look you interrogate the system with your engineers and I'll start watching the four scientists." Felicity confirmed. "There has to be an answer to this and we have to find it soon."

Caton nodded as he leant over his desk and touched the screen in front of him. Four people suddenly appeared on the large, wafer thin screens around the room. The four individuals were all dressed in crisp, white uniforms, there were three men and a woman, the three men were all in their forties and fifties however the woman appeared to be in her early twenties. Felicity glanced at them curiously for a moment as she drew closer to one of the screens and started to inspect each one.

"These are your suspects." Caton announced as he walked towards her and pointed to each one. "They helped me build the system architecture for the Adapt system and if anyone can possibly sabotage it, it would be them."

Felicity nodded. "Names and details please."

"These two, Jacob and Latimer work for a scientific research center on the edge of town, they're pretty stable in that they've worked there for years and are pretty easy to find." Caton explained. "Alessandra on the other hand might be slightly more difficult to track down, she's slightly more elusive and always on the move. Taj, the last I heard, he was working in some top secret, government program. It's highly unlikely he's involved however, he's quite a quiet chap and from what

I know of him, very simple in terms of financial desires and ambitions."

"Great. I'll look into them all." Felicity replied. "This excellent information Caton, now we actually have something to work with."

The meeting concluded as Felicity left and prepared to dig her claws into a deeper, more thorough investigation as she rejoiced that she now had more potential suspects to pursue. Later that morning as she headed back to her office, Caton sent her the four profiles of the scientists he'd identified and she smiled, satisfied with his participation as she received the notification on her phone. She would verify the details of all four suspects by the end of the day and track down each of their whereabouts so that she could monitor each of their movements and interactions more precisely. Surveillance was one of Felicity's strengths and none of the three employees that worked for Caton were even remotely aware that they were being evaluated, monitored and scrutinized further to actually establish whether or not they were responsible for the corporate sabotage or system failures. Her ability to conceal the surveillance operation had meant that their routine had not been disrupted and that they were still fully committed to their work, the company and to their employer Caton.

The need to investigate employees could sometimes cause friction and conflict and Caton had been anxious to avoid this. Felicity knew that he trusted each one of them implicitly and now she felt slightly relieved to actually have other possibilities to consider. Whilst she wanted to investigate all possible suspects, it simply wasn't nice to have to disclose to someone, that they had actually employed and paid an employee that was actually betraying them.

For Genesis the next week seemed to pass by relatively quickly as he engaged with Raccoon and Caton regularly and explored the possibility that perhaps the Adapt system itself could be responsible for the problems the company was facing. They probed the internal back end and spent long hours each evening inspecting each and every program, every loop and every file. It was tedious but necessary as the men searched for answers.

The weekends continued to be lively for Genesis as he filled his nights with passion and sexual liaisons with mysterious females from hotel bars. He indulged fully in his sexual desires which seemed for some reason to be growing as his sexual appetite seemed to change as a result of the mind adaptations he'd implemented into his own brain. During this period, Genesis actually avoided his mother like the plague as he avoided more awkward questions and any explanations he might feel obliged to provide. He worked and played at maximum capacity until he was completely physically worn out and his body actually began to feel slightly burnt out.

The strange man that he'd recognized near his home, he actually noticed on two more occasions, in the quiet empty street he lived in as he'd returned home late in the evenings and walked towards his front door. On the third occasion, Genesis finally decided it was actually time to get a closer look at him and perhaps establish who he actually was. Genesis acted as if he hadn't noticed him as he walked towards his front door and entered inside his home. Once inside however he quickly put on the lights and then slipped out of the back door and made his way quietly around the back of the building. Genesis then quickly walked towards where he had seen the man standing as he slipped his phone out of his pocket.

The curiosity inside him had been pricked and it would not let him rest until he actually knew who this man was and why exactly he was following him or seemed to be. The unanswered question had taunted him for many nights as it had gnawed away at his mind almost like a rat chewing on a piece of rope and now Genesis gripped onto this bone of curiosity with the teeth of bravery as his mind demanded answers. Tonight Genesis was determined he would start to find out exactly what was going on.

SAMARIA

The night's cold air taunted Genesis playfully as he crept around the exterior of his home in the darkness, there were no gardens surrounding his home just a small sidewalk that separated it from the house next door. Genesis walked down it briskly as he quickly pulled the grey jacket he wore around his neck. It was autumn and not quite winter but the cold was starting to enter his world although the freezing temperatures of winter had not quite yet fully arrived. The strange man he quickly found behind a car further along the road as he hide himself in doorways nearby and drew closer. The man's face became clearer as Genesis quickly realized that he'd actually met him at work. He'd been a client who had attended a few sessions and whom Genesis had been assigned to, these facts however still shone no further light on why he was actually standing in the street near his home so late at night or why he was actually following him.   The man continued to stand in the street as he watched his home and made no movement, he neither departed nor drew any closer. Genesis stood in a doorway nearby and watched him for a further fifteen minutes before he finally surrendered to the cold and gave up for the night. Whatever the strange man was actually doing there, Genesis knew he would not be able to establish that night.

By now the warmth of his bed was calling to him and Genesis yearned to embrace it, the mysterious man and his purpose would have to be resolved another day, he quickly decided. He reached for his phone and took a quick photo of the man, the photo would help him match the man with one of the clients on the system he concluded. The photo would also now allow him to actually mention his presence outside his home to Caton.

The next morning when Genesis arrived at work, he booked an appointment to see Caton who wasn't actually available until the next

Friday morning. The two hardly spoke during the weekdays as Genesis attended to clients and when they did usually meet, Genesis was often accompanied by Raccoon and he had no desire to actually hold a sensitive conversation of this nature in Raccoon's presence. Although the presence of the man outside his home troubled Genesis somewhat, the man himself, wasn't necessarily threatening to him and hadn't actually approached him or his home. Genesis quickly started to review the profiles on the Adapt system as he browsed all of his past clients. The man in question, Genesis soon discovered he had actually met a few times and even performed some mind adaptations for him. He had seemed quiet and fairly simple in terms of what he'd asked for and had only actually attended a few follow up sessions. His name was Augustine and Genesis quickly flagged his profile on the system and then turned his attention back to the work he had to actually do that day. When he met with Caton on the Friday, they would discuss the matter further and whatever mystery surrounded Augustine, would then perhaps be resolved.

ADAPTATIONS

The energetic weekends and longer working hours began to take their toll on Genesis's body as he yawned at his desk and it wasn't even the afternoon. He prepared a strong, black coffee and sat back down behind his desk as he drank it. Perhaps he was fooling himself, perhaps it simply wasn't physically viable for his life to continue this way for much longer. Temptation lay strewn across his path however and the urge was hard to resist. The experience of the thrills he'd enjoyed had allowed him to dip his toes into the extreme pleasures available to him through the Adapt system and now as a result, he'd arrived at a crossroads as he wavered on the brink of indecision. Should he continue to live life at full throttle or should he adapt his mind back and slow down the pace once more?

Thoughts ran through the passageways of his mind as he contemplated what he should actually do, he could continue as he was and wear himself out living life to the extremes he had chosen or go backwards and return to his original state to find a more meaningful union or perhaps he thought, he could just modify himself a little and wander closer back towards who he once was more gently, which would still allow him to go further down the path he'd wandered onto but in a slightly more moderate manner. The truth was Genesis had actually enjoyed indulging in exciting casual, sexual liaisons with random women as they'd presented themselves to him and now he was living life a far distance away from the sheltered, monogamous relationship he'd once enjoyed with Cherise. Cherise had actually dumped him though and as much as Genesis had enjoyed their relationship, quite obviously she hadn't.

Each day that week Genesis continued to see his clients and satisfied their requests as he allowed them to explore the manifestations of their desires more fully. Usually he met with Caton each Monday morning for their briefing and at their last briefing Caton had praised him and seemed very impressed with his progress. His client list had grown as his clients recommended him to their friends for various adaptations and Caton was very pleased. Since the system problems had started however, their usual Monday morning meetings were now less frequent and quite often no longer actually occurred but Caton had reassured Genesis at their last meeting around a month ago that he was indeed progressing well and that he was very happy with his output.

"You're good for business Genesis." Caton had remarked with a smile. "Happy clients, referrals, all good things. I like people that are good for my business."

The financial rewards of Genesis's employment had actually started to bless the company coffers and Caton had expressed his appreciation regarding his professionalism and dedication to his job. Genesis often worked late hours whenever there was a need to and he would see new clients at very short notice. Genesis gave clients exactly what they wanted and paid for and was very flexible. He was to Caton the dream employee.

Occasionally Genesis still meet Titus as he continued to fine tune his mind adaptations but Titus was now actually the only client left, from the original list of five clients that Caton had assigned to him. The week progressed as Genesis met with Titus on Wednesday morning just before lunchtime as per his appointment schedule. When they met Titus immediately commented on what he felt was a change in

Genesis's attitude throughout their more recent meetings.

"You seem really different nowadays Genesis." Titus remarked. "Much more confident and relaxed. A new girlfriend perhaps?" He teased playfully.

Genesis shook his head and smiled. "Several possibly too many. I decided to follow in your footsteps for a while and paddle around in the murky waters of casual dating and multiple partners." Genesis replied.

"How's it going? Enjoying it?" Titus enquired curiously.

"Probably a little bit too much, way more than is good for me." Genesis replied.

Their appointment came to an end as Titus glanced at his phone quickly and stood up. He paused for a moment as he looked back at Genesis thoughtfully. "Fancy a spot of lunch?" Titus asked. "Then you can tell me a bit more about your adventures." He teased.

His suggestion was welcomed by Genesis who nodded and stood up. The two men made their way towards the door nearby as they discussed where they should eat and what they both fancied for lunch but arrived at no conclusion.

"Let's just have a wander around and see where we end up." Titus suggested.

Genesis nodded.

A few minutes later as the two men passed through the reception area they smiled at Gemma seated behind the reception desk as they walked past.

"Lunch." Genesis remarked as he opened the exterior door for Titus politely.

Gemma nodded.

It suddenly dawned on Genesis as they exited the building that this was actually the first time since he'd joined the company, that he'd actually ventured outside for lunch. Up until that point in time, he'd simply ordered lunch internally and the kitchen had delivered his meals through the hatch each day as requested.

"Do you think the receptionist would be interested in a little freaky, rough and tumble?" Titus asked as they walked out on the street and the exterior glass doors closed behind them.

"That is one woman that is strictly off limits." Genesis insisted as he playfully pointed a finger at Titus and pretended to scold him.

"You just don't make a mess in places you frequent often. It's not wise."

Titus laughed.

They walked a short distance down the busy streets nearby and soon found themselves in the heart of the bustling city as the discussed women, life and romance cheerfully. They meandered down several more streets, until Titus gently reached for Genesis's arm and led him down a street nearby that he immediately recognized. Titus guided him further along the street and as they approached the restaurant entrance, Genesis's body froze. He quickly realized as panic set in, the eatery that Titus had chosen was none other than the venue of his breakup date with Cherise. Genesis simply couldn't believe it. Titus had actually chosen to take him to lunch in the very same restaurant the love of his life had actually dumped him in. Although they had been heading towards that part of the city Genesis hadn't actually noticed how close they actually were to that particular restaurant as he and Titus had been engrossed in a conversation that had preoccupied his mind and distracted him. They'd discussed various vacations they wanted to have, places they'd never visited that they wanted to see and explore and the reality was Genesis hadn't actually noticed, they'd been gravitating towards that venue until the very last minute and they were right outside the entrance. The two men stood outside the venue for a few seconds as Genesis's body shut down. His obvious hesitation confused Titus as he glanced at Genesis's face a little curiously.

"Are you alright?" Titus asked. "You look a little bit faint."

"I'm fine, I'm fine." Genesis replied. "Just a few bad memories." He paused for a few seconds before he continued. "This restaurant used to be one of my favorite restaurants."

A minute later as the two men walked inside Genesis quickly reassured himself internally that everything was actually going to be fine and that he could handle this. Although he'd managed to convince Titus that there was nothing to worry about, it was quite another to thing to actually convince himself however that the fear he'd aspired to overcome, really could be conquered in reality. Luckily for Genesis as they entered inside, he quickly observed that none of the staff that been working on that dreaded, painful evening were actually in attendance. The horrible evening when Cherise had simply discarded him and he'd been dismissed within five minutes as he'd frustratingly watched his long term relationship be tossed gently into the pile of redundant, unwanted, unrequited love.

A waiter quickly approached the two men as they stood by the reception and seated them quickly. They ordered straight away before the waiter could even hand them the menu tablet he actually carried in his hands as he saved their orders on his device. Genesis didn't even have to look at the menu, he'd seen and studied it so many times by now he actually knew every item on it, he knew exactly what dishes he enjoyed eating there and what exactly he would want to eat for lunch that day. Titus didn't require the menu either and as he clarified his order, the waiter thanked them and departed.

The waiter only disappeared for a few minutes before he returned with two glasses filled with cold beer placed on a tray. He put the glasses of cold beer down on the table in front of them and then departed as he attended to other tables and customers nearby. Genesis watched him scurry away into the distance as they started to drink their chilled beers and talked. Titus was as entertaining as usual and extremely funny as he related more antics to Genesis surrounding some of the activities he'd recently been engaged in.

He listened to Titus politely, intrigued by his stories and laughed at some of the details Titus revealed to him as they waited for their food to arrive. Genesis knew that Titus had actually gone down the road of full, unadulterated, sexual passion and the outcome of his adventures captivated him slightly as he contemplated his own position and the decisions he was now faced with making himself. Some of the stories Titus related to him, Genesis started to realize were now slightly tamer than some of the earlier activities and it suddenly dawned on Genesis that perhaps Titus had calmed down somewhat after the initial frenzy of excitement he'd fully explored. Throughout the peak moments Titus had explored orgies, S & M Parties and partner swapping events but now it appeared that the novelty of extra, additional sexual stimuli seemed to have worn off a little as Titus discussed some of his more recent monogamous, sexual interactions.

The food the two men had ordered arrived shortly after the alcohol as the waiter approached them with stone, black trays filled with lines of meat that sizzled and spat in front of them. He placed the stone slabs filled with meat down on the table in front of them and some other side dishes filled with rice, tangine and other sauces and a plate filled with a variety of breads. The tangine smelt amazing as the aroma filled their nostrils and small chunks of fruit were nestled in some of the pitta breads, bowls that contained a variety of chutney's and sauces lay scattered across the table as the two men sat up and prepared to devour the delicious treats in front of them. They thanked the waiter and he quickly departed as they hungrily attacked the food in front of them. They ripped off chunks of bread and dipped them into the tangine and other sauce filled bowls in front of them as they began to fill their empty stomachs with the tantalizing morsels of food.

The delicious meal was over all too quickly as both men sat back and relaxed for a moment once they'd had their fill, content and satisfied with the culinary delights that the restaurant had presented. Only a few minutes went by however before Titus suddenly seemed to become distracted as Genesis watched him glance at a nearby table curiously. Titus stood up and winked at Genesis.

"I'll be back in a few minutes." Titus explained. "The little boys room." He continued in almost like a whisper.

There was nothing unusual about his remark and Genesis nodded politely as Titus headed off towards the nearby restroom. Genesis started to play around with his phone for a few minutes as he thought about Cherise. He couldn't help it, he'd been left alone in the very venue she'd dumped him in and the memories began to resurface. He quickly found himself sinking into thoughts surrounding their breakup as he replayed the events of that awful night over and over again in his mind and gazed at the bar stool he'd actually been seated on when she'd actually dumped him. Time seemed to pass by very slowly as Genesis glanced at a clock on the nearby wall and realized that it had actually been ten minutes since Titus had left him alone seated at the table to go to the bathroom. Just as Genesis began to feel slightly impatient about his absence however Titus returned. Genesis looked at him with a puzzled expression as Titus sat back down.

"She's what took me so long." Titus explained as he smiled and nodded towards a brunette seated at a table nearby with a much older, more mature man. "On the way back from the gents, I went on a slight detour with her, into one of the ladies cubicles."

"You didn't?" Genesis whispered back as he smiled and shook his head in disbelief.

"I did. She got down on her knees for me. I'm very satisfied." He explained. "Her mouth was very enjoyable. Great desert."

His comments surprised Genesis as his eyes widened with disbelief, however a few seconds later when the woman in question suddenly glanced over at Titus and smiled at him and he reciprocated with a wink, it was clear to see that there was definitely grain of truth in what he had actually said.

"I have her number." Titus explained in a quiet voice to Genesis. "We're going to meet later tonight and finish what we started."

The waiter interrupted their conversation as he arrived back at the table with the bill and Genesis laughed as he digested Titus's remarks. Titus had totally surprised him and caught him off guard and no matter how much he tried to imagine such things ever happening to him, he simply couldn't. Titus paid the bill quickly and the two men left. Once they reached the street outside they continued to discuss the woman Titus had explored intimately inside the ladies toilets together as they walked.

"Weren't you a bit scared? I mean you had to actually go inside the ladies toilets." Genesis teased playfully. "I would have been terrified. You just don't go in there. Not ever."

"I was for a second and then I just thought, if anyone asks me why I'm in there, I'll just say she needed some kind of urgent assistance." Titus replied in a very serious tone.

Genesis smiled at his ingenuity and quick thinking.

The two men continued to walk and talk and as they neared the end of the street as the topic leant towards the issue of Genesis's love life. He started to share with Titus some brief details of recent sexual adventures he'd enjoyed as they walked. Distracted and consumed by the conversation Genesis didn't actually notice a woman suddenly darted out of the doorway of a shop nearby as she headed straight towards him, her arms laden with shopping bags. She bumped straight into Genesis as both parties failed to avoid the collision due to their lack of attention to the sidewalk and their surroundings. Genesis turned to face her immediately with an apologetic expression on his face as he leant down towards the ground quickly and helped her pick up some of her bags and the items strewn across the ground.

"I'm so sorry." Genesis muttered as he glanced up at her face for a moment. His hands by now were filled some of the items that had been strewn across the sidewalk just a few seconds before as he placed them back into the shopping bags carefully.

"It's ok, its ok. It was totally my fault." A soft, sensual, familiar, feminine voice replied.

The voice was not the only thing that was familiar as Genesis glanced up at her face, the face Genesis also recognized immediately as he smiled with surprise. "You again." Genesis remarked playfully as he looked into the soft, hazel, green eyes that met his. "We really must stop bumping into each other like this." He teased.

"We really must." Samaria replied as she laughed gently.

The two continued to crouch close to the ground as they picked up the remaining tins and packets of food, that were scattered across the sidewalk and placed them back into the bags quickly, that they'd been securely nestled inside prior to their collision. Titus stood quietly at the side of the sidewalk a few steps away as he watched them, not daring to interrupt what was so obviously an intimate conversation between Genesis and a woman he already knew in some capacity.

"Can I take you out for a coffee perhaps one day?" Genesis suggested. "It'll be much more fun than these unplanned, random collisions, that sometimes result in breakages. I promise." He teased.

The two stood up and faced each other as Samaria smiled at him.

"Definitely." Samaria agreed.

The positive response pleased Genesis and he quickly fished a business card out of his trouser pocket and handed it to her. "I'm Genesis." He said as he smiled.

"I know, you told me your name last time we met. Well last time we bumped into each other." Samaria replied as she smiled. "I remember."

"Right and you're Samaria right?" Genesis asked politely as he prayed inside that he'd actually remembered her name correctly. Woman weren't usually impressed by men who forgot their names, it usually implied a lack of interest.

Samaria nodded.

"I'm very single right now so you can call me any time, day or night." Genesis clarified as he sought to ascertain clearly that he definitely had a romantic interest in her. "Are you single?"

The question jumped out from behind his lips as he decided to quickly check on her availability before he actively, actually pursued her any further as the issue of her singleness suddenly became extremely important. Unlike most of the women he'd met recently in the hotel bars he'd frequented, who he'd been perfectly happy to jump into bed with regardless of their marital status, suddenly for some reason Samaria's marital status seemed to matter. She seemed to matter.

Samaria smiled at him warmly. "I'm very single right now." She continued as she tucked his card away inside one of the interior pockets of her handbag. "I'll definitely call you. I'd better go I have to go back to work." Samaria explained. "And I think your friend is waiting for you." She teased.

Her remark suddenly reminded Genesis of Titus's presence as he suddenly glanced at him and smiled. He'd almost forgotten Titus was there, he'd been so wrapped up in his conversation with Samaria and lost in the excitement of actually meeting her again. He felt slightly guilty about it for a second as he smiled at Titus slightly apologetically. Titus shook his head and waved his hand at him as if to reassure him that he didn't actually mind and to encourage him to go ahead. Samaria smiled at Genesis as he looked into her eyes. Invisible fingers and arms seemed to wrap themselves around Genesis's body and comfort him and it almost seemed as if somehow her presence and close proximity was warming his body internally. He felt strangely drawn to her, for someone inexplicable reason. She intrigued him and he was captivated. She'd fully captured his attention in a way that no other woman had for a while. No other woman, since Cherise.

"I really have to go." Samaria explained as she glanced down at her phone and quickly realized that her lunch break was almost over. "My boss can be very unforgiving if I get return late."

Genesis nodded as he watched her depart and walk away from him. She might call, she might not, their future now lay in her hands and only she could actually decide whether there would be one or not.

Titus drew closer to Genesis as he slapped him gently on the back and smiled at him playfully. The two men smiled at each other and then started to make their way back across the city streets as they headed back towards the New Minds Inc. building. Lunch was well and truly over for Genesis and he had some client appointments he actually had to prepare for that afternoon.

"She's pretty." Titus remarked as they walked. "She has very unusual eyes."

"She is and she does." Genesis agreed. "I met her a while ago but I was very involved with another woman at the time and very committed so I didn't pursue anything further with her at the time." Genesis explained. "I thought I was going to get married."

"Ok to the one who gave you bad memories?" Titus teased. "Good thing your single now right?"

Genesis smiled and nodded. "Let's hope so." He replied.

The two men soon arrived back outside the New Minds Inc. building and bade each other farewell as Genesis thanked Titus for lunch. He'd returned slightly later than planned but it had been worth it, he thought as he prepared to return to his consultation room and leave Titus's side. Titus was fun and sometimes, Genesis actually needed to have fun, he decided.

"Until next time." Titus remarked playfully as he glanced at the time on his phone. "I have to get back to the trading floor, then later today I have to fulfill a special, urgent order and meet this lady's needs. I left her hungry and thirsty and it's my duty to quench that and satisfy her appetite completely."

His remark prompted a smile to appear on Genesis's face as Titus slapped him gently on the back and then disappeared rapidly down one of the side roads nearby. The woman, Titus had referred to was quite obviously, the woman he'd met in the restaurant and slipped into the toilets with and Genesis knew from Titus's remark the interaction earlier that day between them both was far from over. Genesis's cheeks shone as he walked into the reception and smiled at Gemma, he felt totally refreshed. It was good to go out for lunch sometimes.

"How was lunch?" Gemma asked curiously as Genesis passed her desk.

"Great thanks Gemma." Genesis replied as he smiled at her before he quickly headed through the interior glass doors nearby that led towards the elevator.

Thoughts of Samaria danced through Genesis's mind as he walked and speculated as to whether she would actually call him later that day. He'd actually enjoyed bumping into Samaria again and the painful experience of eating lunch in the same restaurant where Cherise had dumped him had by now been totally forgotten and replaced by feelings of appreciation regarding how fate had brought them together once more at exactly the right moment in time. The reality was if Genesis had actually met Samaria again right after his break up with Cherise, the results of any relationship between them would quite simply, probably have been a mess and Genesis knew it. Rebounds after a broken heart were usually a disaster and Genesis's heart had been well and truly broken. Deep inside he knew, he'd have probably tried to inflict the pain that Cherise had bestowed upon him onto someone else and he'd have probably devastated Samaria's life also in the process. Perhaps there was some kind of force of fate or God, Genesis decided, who brought the right people into your life at precisely the right time, in order to provide you with the lessons and nourishment you needed. He'd never exactly been a religious person or even superstitious but his recent encounter with Samaria now prompted him to challenge his lack of belief in anything he couldn't touch, see, smell or feel as he clung onto the moment and enjoyed the pleasant surprise of meeting her once again.

The conversational exchange and meeting had also refreshed Samaria as she walked back towards the fashion house in the heart of the city that she worked for, her arms laden with full shopping bags. Genesis had quite simply been one of the one's that got away and although she'd thought about him a few times since they're first collision, Samaria had never actually believed in the possibility that they would ever met again. Millions of people lived in Mansfield, a city that quite simply never slept and that housed at least fifty million people. The chances of meeting Genesis again had been very remote and she'd pushed the thought of doing so to the back of her mind as something that was very unlikely to actually happen.

For some strange reason however, the two had met again and in almost the same place they'd originally met the first time. Samaria smiled as she glanced down at his business card that now sat in the palm of her hand and vowed to call him. It was rare that one was given the chance to actually correct a mistake that they had made in the past and even more rare that such a mistake could be corrected with the same person and extremely rare that strangers would be able to meet again in such unusual circumstances. An opportunity however had presented itself once more and this time Samaria would not allow it to slip through her fingertips. Genesis was not going to be just another participant in her wishful thinking about the life she could have had and the things she could have enjoyed. She tucked the business card away once more into the pocket of her handbag and then turned her focus back towards work, she'd call him later that evening, she decided, once she was in the privacy of her own home and could speak more freely. She'd give him her number, encourage him and allow him to pursue her romantically and then see where things went. Since the two had last met, she hadn't even dated and that urgently needed to change, for her sake and for the sake of all her female friends who were bored to death of hearing about her single status and pushing her to indulge in romantic affairs.

Unusually, later that afternoon once Genesis had settled back into work, Caton visited his consultation room. The sudden appearance of Caton struck Genesis with surprise as he absolutely never attended his consultation room without a prior appointment. Genesis showed him inside the room and Caton sat down. His consultation room was actually empty as Genesis's first appointment wasn't due to begin until a bit later that afternoon and Genesis smiled as he sat down and faced Caton and prepared for their conversation.

"I know we had an appointment for Friday morning Genesis, but something's come up and I really can't make it." Caton explained. "Can we do it today instead?" He asked politely.

Genesis nodded and quickly loaded the image of Augustine onto the screen in front of him and then displayed the profile on one of the wafer thin screens on the wall nearby. "This man, Augustine has been following me." Genesis explained. "I'm not sure why. I've seen him in the street near my home a few times late at night. He was one of my clients."

Caton nodded as he absorbed the details of what Genesis said and inspected the client's profile. "How often has this happened and when?" Caton asked. "Recently?"

"It's actually happened about five or six times now, usually very late at night around midnight." Genesis explained. "It's very strange."

"Could he live in the same street as you do or be visiting a friend, relative or lover perhaps?" Caton asked him politely as he sought out a logical explanation for Augustine's presence.

"I'm not sure. I haven't seen him entering into a house or leaving any of the houses in the street." Genesis replied. "I'd have to watch the street I live in or something to find out. I usually get home quite late so it's impossible to tell really. The worst part is I actually gave him mind adaptations to enable him to be more ruthless. He's a hit man and he asked me to increase his levels of courage and reduce his levels of empathy so that he could perform his job more effectively."

Caton 's eyebrows raised in surprise.

"Do you think someone's put a hit out on me?" Genesis asked a little nervously.

"I doubt it Genesis." Caton reassured him. "It's probably nothing at all. Anyway thanks for letting me know, I'll look into it." He insisted as he stood up and walked towards the door. "It could be nothing at all but it's best I just make sure anyway."

Genesis felt immediately reassured as Caton stood up and left the room. Whoever this man was, Caton would find out.

The remainder of the afternoon evaporated slowly as Genesis watched the hours pass impatiently, anxious to return home and wait for Samaria's call. For once, unusually, he was actually opposed to staying at work as late as he possibly could, to avoid the emptiness and loneliness of his home. Today he actually wanted to return home as soon as possible. Work and the recent long hours due to the system problems had provided a sufficient distraction to Genesis and kept him busy, but today he didn't actually want to busy, he wanted to be at home, available and ready to receive the call, that may change his dreary, single status and give him someone to care about once more. Each second seemed to drag by as Genesis waited and waited, why was it he mused, when you wanted time to go by very quickly, it actually never did and yet when you wanted it to actually last longer and pass more slowly, it disappeared in a flash? It was almost as if time had somehow forged a deal against humanity, a deal where time disappeared as quickly as possible, the more people were enjoying themselves and then drew itself out painfully slowly, when people were engaged in doing something they hated or waiting for something exciting to happen.

Genesis attended to his clients as he focused on his tasks and tried to forget about the potential phone call he might receive from

Samaria for a while. Luckily for him the mind adaptations work he was actually employed to perform was very engaging and the clients he met with often presented him with challenges, that he often had to research more thoroughly. The nature of his engaging work had often a blessing, that had carried him through each day and kept him well and truly occupied and once more it faithfully distracted him as he focused on his clients and took his mind of the time.

When the clock eventually hit six, Genesis jumped up enthusiastically as he switched off the computer in front of him and then headed towards the door. Excitement surged through his veins although he knew he actually wouldn't see Samaria that day, her call and the sound of her voice would be enough to satisfy the thirst her presence in his life had now created. Once Genesis arrived at the reception area, he found that Gemma had already abandoned her desk and been replaced by the night shift security guard and the two men nodded at each other as Genesis walked towards the exterior front door and prepared to leave the building. Tonight he would actually pursue something different he thought, something more than the seedy, shady affairs he'd indulged so frequently recently, tonight he would start to pursue a proper relationship once again, with a woman he actually desired more than a quick fumble in the dark with. He stepped out of the exterior door and as he did so Genesis walked out on the casual, quick, purely sexual experiences he'd sought out as he left behind the short, sexual liaisons with strangers. The steps he took as he walked out of the door, illustrated his mental steps as he walked towards a deeper, more committed, romantic, loving relationship once again.

The building fell silent as the security night watchman watched Genesis leave, this quietness was short-lived however as it was disturbed a few minutes later by Caton.

He walked into the reception area and smiled at the night watchman as he approached the reception desk. "Everyone gone?" He asked politely.

"Yes sir." The quiet security guard replied.

"Good. I have a visitor this evening." Caton verified. "They should be here shortly."

Caton was relieved that for once that all of the employees that usually occupied the building had today abandoned it relatively early in the evening and actually returned to their homes. Due to the recent system problems, Raccoon and Genesis usually worked late most evenings even after most of the consultants had left, but for some reason today, they'd actually decided not to. That for once suited Caton as he'd organized a meeting with Felicity and actually agreed to show her around the whole building as part of her investigation. The less people there were around to question why she was inspecting each room, the less of a problem it was to both him and her. They both felt it was in their best interests to keep as much of the investigation as confidential as possible, until the situation had actually been resolved. At the employee briefing she'd simply been introduced as a security specialist, not as an actual investigator and Caton wanted to retain that perception amongst his staff. He did not want his employees to feel uncomfortable or as if they were under any kind of suspicion as it would disturb the services they provided to his clientele.

Minutes walked through the air and disappeared as Caton waited patiently inside the reception area until Felicity messaged his phone to let him know she was actually outside in the parking lot. A few minutes later when she met Caton by the exterior door, he unlocked it briskly and then let her inside the building as he smiled at her. The two then walked down the hallway nearby as they headed towards his office briskly. Caton, unable to wait until they actually arrived inside his office began to probe Felicity further on how things were progressing as he enquired about the four scientists he'd mentioned to her at their previous meeting.

"Did you manage to find them all?" Caton enquired as he quizzed her impatiently.

"Yes. All except one. Jacob, Latimer and Taj were relatively easy to find and were exactly where you said they would be. Alessandra on the other hand was slightly more tricky to track down." Felicity explained. "It appears she now might be operating under a entirely different name and identity altogether. I'm really not sure. I'm still working on that one."

Caton seemed satisfied as he led Felicity into his office and she sat down at his desk. "Hungry?" Caton asked.

Felicity nodded.

"I'll get a local restaurant to fix us some food and deliver it." Caton explained as he touched the screen in front of him and started to access a food menu. "All the kitchen staff have gone home already." He explained. "What do you fancy, steak, grilled fish, salad?"

"Can I have a steak please?" Felicity asked.

"Certainly." Caton replied as he nodded. Caton touched the screen in front of him and ordered the food that the both wanted as the order was submitted straight into a local restaurant's order line.

"I think you might want to look into this guy." Caton mentioned as he touched the screen in front of him once more and Augustine's image appeared on the wafer, thin screens on the walls nearby. "He's been spotted following one of our staff around and has actually been sighted near his home quite a few times late at night." Caton explained. "We saw him briefly for a while as a client."

"Any idea who he is?" Felicity ventured.

"None at all." Caton replied as he shook his head. "Don't recognize the face and have absolutely no idea who he could be. Just thought I'd bring him to your attention in case it's important."

Felicity nodded as she plucked a small, black device out of the small, black briefcase she carried around with her. A few seconds later the man's face and image appeared on the device in her hands as she smiled and nodded at Caton. "I've got his details now. I'll do a bit of digging around." She verified.

SEEKING REDEMPTION

The evening dawned as the dusky darkness started to fall down upon the city as Genesis drove across the quiet back streets towards his home, he had no desire to be stuck in traffic jams, not this evening and had opted for the back roads instead as he'd made his way toward the phone call he expected. He stopped off at a fast food joint and picked up a pizza on his way then he rushed home to relax for the evening. An hour later as he flicked through the channels available on the large screen on the wall situated in the lounge, his phone finally rang and he answered it eagerly as he picked it up from the coffee table nearby with a smile on his lips. A few seconds later a sensual, sweet, feminine voice greeted him and he sighed with relief as he realized, it was definitely Samaria.

"Hi Genesis. I'd just thought I'd give you a call before you forget who I am." Samaria explained as she greeted him.

"I'm so glad you did." Genesis replied. "When can I take you out for that coffee I promised you?" He asked.

There was a slight pause for a moment as Samaria quietly considered her schedule for a few minutes before she responded. Genesis waited patiently for a response but none was forthcoming so he started to make suggestions in an attempt to be more flexible.

"We could always go for lunch tomorrow." He suggested. "That's if you're free."

The suggestion was welcomed by Samaria who had been considering whether or not she could actually attend an evening appointment, hence her hesitation. Evening appointments could be tricky for her at times as she had to collect her daughter Charlotte from the minder, who picked her up from school each day and quite often she finished work quite late in the evenings, which often meant she had to rush. During the week days, Samaria worked in an extremely popular, busy fashion house as a designers assistant, a job which rarely spared her a break aside from the hour's lunch that she took routinely every day at around one in the afternoon. She often left work around 7 p.m. each day and there was little scope for additional appointments especially not those which involved leisure activities. There were various functions and catwalk shows she also often had to attend after her usual working hours which meant that the child minder often had to assist her with Charlotte's after school care and meeting Genesis throughout one of the weekday evenings was virtually impossible.

"I can make it at one 'o' clock." Samaria suggested, excited by the prospect that Genesis actually wanted to meet so soon.

"Great I'll see you then." Genesis confirmed.

The lunch date was agreed as Samaria accepted that this time, Genesis had not passed her by and that the opportunity to get to know him had actually presented itself again. Samaria hadn't actually dated anyone for a while and since she'd bumped into Genesis that very first time, she'd often thought about what it may be like to actually go on a date with him. Now she would actually find out.

Violet her best friend knew all about Genesis and their random collision as she'd explained it to her last time they'd met. Violet had teased Samaria about her lack of action and the fact that there had been no forthcoming date from their first meeting as she'd explained to her the events of their first collision to her and told her about the first evening she'd actually bumped into Genesis.

"I met an extremely handsome, charming, stranger." Samaria had explained to Violet whilst they had been on an outing with their children to the zoo.

The two women both had children around the same age and had been friends for years and their children, Charlotte and Danny had formed a steadfast friendship, that complimented their own. They were comfortable with each other and over the years they'd developed a deep bond of trust. Violet unlike Samaria however was a little more outgoing, a little more confident and a little more assertive, especially when it came to the issue of men.

"What happened did you get his number?" Violet had asked curiously as she'd started to tease her and press for more of the juicy details.

"I didn't" Samaria had replied a little dejected that she hadn't had a longer conversation with Genesis and that nothing substantial had actually arisen from their meeting.

"When you want something in this life, you have to go for it." Violet had insisted as they stood in the dusty, giraffe enclosure. The floor around them was scattered with sawdust and straw as they watched Danny and Charlotte laugh at one of the giraffe's pulling a face nearby and smiled. "You have to smile more, flirt more, be more confident." She'd insisted. "You are a very beautiful woman. Be proud of that. Be proud of you."

Her encouraging comments had reassured Samaria, who had nodded in response and accepted her advice. Reality for her was very different however in that unlike Violet she simply wasn't as confident and was definitely less flirtatious and these shortcomings seemed to hamper her dating life. The personal setbacks she faced, seemed to have an impact as she froze whenever she was actually around a male that she found physically attractive. She was very focused on her job and role as a mother to Charlotte, both of which consumed a lot of her time and that meant she simply didn't have that much time to give dating much consideration and the little time she did have, just didn't seem to provide any kind of productive results. She had tried to excuse her failings as she'd explained herself further to Violet that day.

"There really wasn't time Violet, we just bumped into each other unexpectedly on the street." Samaria had explained as she attempted to justify her position and her lack of action.

"A few seconds is all you really need Samaria, a smile, a touch of the hand, a positive signal of interest. If you see him again make sure you make the most of the occasion." Violet had insisted as she rejected her excuses and dismissed them immediately.

The final response had been met by silence from Samaria as she'd surrendered to her observations. Violet unlike Samaria, was much more forward and outgoing and she always had a good looking date on her arm and a list of eligible men she could call on at any time to take her anywhere she wanted to go, whenever she desired male companionship. Unlike some other women however who were more confident and outgoing, Violet was not actually promiscuous and she took her time before she actually jumped into bed with any man or explored any kind of sexual intimacy with them.

The two women who'd been friends since college had a deep founded respect for each other and their friendship had been nurtured, developed and grown over the years. Samaria listened to Violet's opinions and often shared her own as they'd assisted each other to overcome the obstacles that life presented to them both. Between the two women Samaria was the quieter, shy one of the two and she often envied the confidence Violet seemed to possess, especially when it came to the issue of the opposite sex. Their two children, Danny and Charlotte as a result of their own deep friendship had also developed a bond, which sometimes seemed almost as deep as that of a biological brother and sister.

Once Samaria had finished speaking to Genesis, she quickly rang Violet to let her know that she'd actually met Genesis again and that this time she actually had his phone number and that they would be meeting for a lunch date. Violet was excited as she answered the phone and Samaria explained the situation to her.

"If you need a baby sitter at any time for a weekend date just let me know." Violet teased. "Charlotte can even stay with us for the whole weekend." She suggested playfully.

"Thanks but I think it's a bit early for that." Samaria replied as she sat in the huge, dark, grey sofa inside her lounge and sipped on a cup of piping, hot coffee as they'd talked.

"Come on, you haven't had it for absolutely ages." Violet teased in response. "You need to relieve some of the sexual frustration inside you or your body will be filled with tension."

Her suggestion prompted a smile to appear on Samaria's face as she giggled and reflected on the grains of truth scattered within Violet's observations. The comments were definitely accurate, Samaria thought as she quickly realized it had actually been at least a year since she'd last indulged in sexual activities with anyone. She quietly yearned for a moment to be held and wrapped in Genesis's strong arms as she wondered what it might be like to actually spend a night with him.

Samaria shook her head quickly as she pulled herself out of the fantasy and firmly back down to earth.

"There's no rush Violet." Samaria replied. "It'll happen when it's supposed to. We'll get naked when it's the right time."

"Wimp." Violet teased as she laughed at her.

"We're not all love troopers, who go charging in when it comes to the bedroom, some of us like to meander in gently, like a stream gurgling along a familiar bed, rather than a tidal wave crashing against the shores of an unknown beach." She explained.

"Let me know when you're ready." Violet insisted as she quickly pushed her excuses and deliberations to one side, like an unwanted item of food on a plate. "He won't wait forever. Once you fall of the horse you have to get back on it or you'll end up like a dusty book covered in cobwebs, forgotten and ignored, sitting at the top of the bookshelf out of everyone's sight and reach." Violet teased.

The next day Samaria prepared for work as usual but also for her lunch date with Genesis as she inspected the drab interior of her wardrobe glumly and searched for something appropriate to wear. She contemplated some of the comments Violet had made a little further as she surrendered to the fact that Violet was definitely right and that her wardrobe even reflected that. Dating wasn't something she'd even thought about doing for a very long time and even her wardrobe had started to reflect this. The contents of her closet were unattractive and mainly formal, she thought as she rummaged through them, too formal for a date. Luckily however just as she was about to give up, she managed to eventually find a slightly, sophisticated, black and white dress hanging quietly at the rear. It was a dress she'd been given from a fashion show that she'd attended over a year ago and she'd absolutely never worn it before as she hadn't been anywhere that justified the effort.

A clothes shopping trip was definitely required soon Samaria thought as she took the dress of the hanger enthusiastically and held it up against her body. The dress was totally perfect, smart enough for work, flattering and figure hugging enough for a date and as she slipped it on, it's shape accentuated her curves. Luckily it was not too revealing, which meant it could actually be worn to work comfortably. No one would actually ever guess that she actually worked in a fashion house, Samaria thought as she glanced at the interior of her wardrobe, its contents definitely didn't reflect the glamorous outfits she often handled every day as part of her job.

On the other side of the city, Genesis prepared for his day as he pulled a smarter than usual, pair of trousers and shirt from his closet and started to dress. He splashed some aftershave onto his neck and then placed then whole bottle inside his work briefcase for later that morning, he'd definitely need it again he thought. By the time lunchtime arrived, he quickly calculated the effects of the aftershave would have worn off and the aroma dulled somewhat and he'd need to then reapply it before he left the office to meet Samaria, in order to create an amazing impression upon her at lunch that day.

Once dressed Genesis quickly left his home as he eagerly made his way through the city backstreets and headed to work. The drive was shorter than usual as he was slightly early which meant the roads were less hectic as the heavy morning traffic had not yet started to swamp the roads. By actually leaving a little earlier that morning he'd been spared the irritation of waiting at traffic lights that would change several times before the long lines of cars managed to proceed. The usual stifled, cramped crawl, that usually accompanied him on his journey to work, he managed to successfully avoid by leaving home an hour earlier than usual. Genesis's plan was to arrive at work slightly earlier that morning as that would then entitle him to the flexibility of a slightly longer lunch break than usual, just in case the need arose. Caton wasn't a strict boss and as long as employees saw all their clients and attended work for the required hours each week, he was quite flexible about how they actually managed their day and lunch breaks.

Thirty minutes later as Genesis arrived inside his consultation room, he began to contemplate how his recent mind adaptations and personality changes may affect any relationship he might have with Samaria as he prepared for his first appointment that day. He definitely wasn't the same loyal, devoted, faithful man that had once been so dedicated to Cherise and he knew it, he'd changed, the mind adaptations had changed him.

ADAPTATIONS

The first client he was due to see that morning arrived as he pushed his thoughts to one side and made his way quickly downstairs to meet him. The man in question a large framed man called Justin, sat on the sofa in the reception area as he waited for him quietly. Genesis greeted him and then quickly escorted him back to his consultation room as he sought to fulfill his requirements and then prepare for lunch. Luckily that morning, Genesis only had one client appointment which meant he had more than sufficient time to actually prepare himself and make his way towards the agreed meeting place for his lunch date. The venue they'd both agreed on was actually situated on the opposite side of the city and that was another reason he'd actually attended work earlier than usual. It would take time to get there and back and an hour's lunch break simply wouldn't suffice.

Justin cleared his throat as he prepared to respond to Genesis's questions regarding the mind adaptations he required. "I'd really like to be much more friendly." Justin explained as he faced him. "Due to my size and weight, many people find me intimidating." He continued. "They find it hard to relate to me."

Although it seemed to be a simple request and something Genesis thought he would be able to resolve relatively easily, Justin seemed very sincerely troubled, frustrated and deeply concerned by the dilemma his physicality actually presented as he fidgeted nervously. Genesis tried to help him relax.

"This is not a huge problem." Genesis insisted as he attempted to reassure him that he could help him. "By adapting your personality, we'll make you more approachable." He continued as he loaded his profile onto the screen in front of him and prepared to attend to his needs as he started to analyze his brain. It wasn't hard for Genesis to find an optimal solution relatively quickly and he suggested one as soon as he'd identified the correct personality traits to adapt. "I'd like to increase your levels of confidence slightly." Genesis suggested. "And increase your gentleness." He remarked.

"Can you really do that?" Justin asked. "If you could do that, I think that would be great." He continued as he nodded enthusiastically. "I feel very socially isolated right now. I mean I really struggle to make friends as people are just kind of scared of me."

ADAPTATIONS

"This is not a huge problem." Genesis insisted reassuringly as he started to make the relevant adjustments to his mind personality traits on the screen in front of him. "It's a very simple mind adaptation to perform."

Whilst Genesis worked, his mind continued to meander into thoughts surrounding his pending lunch meeting with Samaria as the distracting thoughts teased him playfully and provoked him. They seemed to run through the passages of his mind, tap on the doors of deeper contemplation and then run away as soon as he opened them, the unknown events of his date that lay on the horizon of events yet to occur continue to taunt him seductively as he tried to be disciplined and focus on the task at hand. Justin interrupted his thoughts several times as he demanded his attention quite frequently throughout their consultation. The interruptions brought Genesis back down to earth very quickly and deterred him from wandering to deeply into his own thoughts and from becoming to distracted with his own plans.

When the consultation finally concluded and Genesis had satisfied Justin's request, he then escorted him back down to the reception area and watched him depart. Once he'd gone Genesis quickly made his way back upstairs and prepared for his lunch meeting with Samaria excitedly as he leapt into his consultation room and headed straight for his bottle of aftershave. Due to the fact that the two worked at opposite ends of the city, they'd actually planned to meet at a venue situated slightly closer to Samaria's workplace as her lunch schedule was slightly tighter and less flexible than Genesis's was. Before he left Genesis quickly grabbed his toothbrush and toothpaste from his bag and made his way into the bathroom adjacent to his consultation room as he made his final preparations for the lunch date ahead.

Enthusiasm and excitement gripped Genesis's body as he made his way towards the eatery where he'd reserved a table for his lunch date with Samaria. It wasn't extremely lavish but it was comfortable and the food and service was excellent. A short, bald waiter greeted Genesis at the door as soon as he arrived and then quickly showed him to a table nearby, situated near the entrance as he talked away excessively.

"Here's a menu." He said enthusiastically as soon as Genesis was seated as he handed him a large menu that he'd been carrying under his arm.

The long winded speech he'd just ended about the weather in various parts of the world, that he'd digressed into as soon as Genesis had arrived, sounded a little rehearsed and as if it was something he actually, usually said to every customer he met. Genesis smiled and thanked him politely, grateful that he'd now actually concluded the one sided conversation that Genesis was not at all remotely interested in and that it was over. Luckily Genesis didn't have to wait very long for Samaria as she arrived five minutes later. Genesis smiled and stared at her as she entered inside the venue, captivated by her beauty. Samaria looked absolutely stunning as she walked towards him. Whilst Samaria didn't have the sleek, slim, model shaped frame that Cherise possessed and the cosmetically, perfect face to match it, her body was slightly more voluptuous and possessed some very enticing curves. Her face had a cute prettiness, that was unusual and unique and the combination of her face and body together was extremely attractive.

In comparison to Cherise, her appearance to Genesis was equally sufficient and perhaps even a slightly more than satisfying equivalent. Genesis hadn't been shortchanged at all after his loss he quickly concluded, this was a woman that his mother would definitely approve of and even quite possibly even like. Cherise wasn't the end of his dating life after all, now there was hope that someone else could actually fill the gap that her absence had created. He stood up quickly, to acknowledge her presence as Samaria made her way towards the table at which he was seated. He kissed her cheek gently as she drew closer to him and they both smiled as they sat down at the table. They were interrupted a few seconds later by the waiter, who had noticed her arrival and rushed over to attend to them both.

"What can I get you?" The short, bald, talkative man asked as he stood by the table in front of them.

"I'd like a steak." Genesis replied politely, almost immediately as if he wanted to put the waiter out of his misery. Such a question,

Genesis knew would often result in a prolonged silence as customers deliberated over the menu and being a talkative kind of waiter, such a silence would probably be quite unbearable for him. "What would you like to eat Samaria?" Genesis prompted as he turned to face her. "Order anything you like, it's my treat." He urged as he smiled at her. The sooner Samaria had actually ordered, the sooner the waiter would depart and the sooner they would be alone once more, he thought.

Although Genesis appreciate the attentive service that the waiter provided, he wished to avoid any gabbling, irrelevant conversation, the waiter might attempt to make as he waited for them to make a decision. Even though it was polite, it was also slightly irritating.

A few seconds later Samaria made a commitment and selected two dishes, a starter and a main from the menu as she smiled. "I think I'd like the skewered, barbecue prawns please and the red, Thai, chicken curry with rice." She replied.

The waiter nodded and scribbled down their requests quickly, he then picked up the menu's a few seconds later and departed as he left the two alone once more. Genesis began to relax as he filled their glasses with some wine and the conversation between them began to flow. The lunch date lasted roughly about an hour and by the time they left the restaurant Genesis was truly besotted with Samaria. The conversation and atmosphere between them had been tantalizing and he quite simply couldn't accept leaving her presence without making another date at some point in the very near future.

He pressed Samaria eagerly to commit to another date before she actually departed. "Let's meet on Friday." He suggested eagerly as they stood just outside the eatery on the busy city street. "We can go for dinner and then watch a movie."

Samaria looked him thoughtfully for a moment as she considered her circumstances further. Whilst she wanted to say yes to Genesis immediately, she also knew that it was wiser in the long run to actually prolong her decision slightly. She wanted to avoid giving Genesis the impression that she had no other priorities, when she clearly knew she had and could not simply drop everything for him whenever he wanted her too. She was a mother and Charlotte was her first responsibility, not dating Genesis.

"I'll have to check with my daughter's minder first." Samaria clarified as she attempted to communicate clearly and honestly to Genesis, the fact that her life wasn't as simple as his and that she indeed had other responsibilities that came first.

Deep within Samaria actually knew that she had several possible minders for Charlotte that would be more than willing to babysit for her, even at short notice but she wanted to make sure that Genesis didn't take her availability for granted. Meeting Genesis again was indeed a blessing but even though he was handsome and in the midst of sweeping her off her feet, she wanted to make sure he understood her life and circumstances from the very beginning. Samaria wasn't a freely, available, single woman and that fact had to be made crystal clear from the outset, so that it didn't lead to more complicated misunderstandings in the future. Genesis was a very single man and Samaria could tell that he probably had no idea what the reality of raising a child actually meant and what the impact of doing so actually had on one's life.

Whilst her response delayed the agreement of a second date slightly, it didn't actually put Genesis off at all as he smiled. He quickly reminded himself, that Samaria was indeed a mother and that she had actually given birth to a child that she was actually raising alone. He admired her strength and courage to do so and then contemplated for a moment why she might actually be doing so as he glanced into her soft, gentle eyes. Genesis smiled as he pushed the niggling questions to the back of his mind abruptly, now was not the right time to raise that topic, he quickly decided. The relationship between them was still a newborn baby itself and not yet even a toddler and he had absolutely no desire whatsoever to push Samaria into disclosing what could be complex, murky details from her past, that she might not be actually comfortable discussing with him yet.

"Let me know." Genesis replied as he smiled and nodded enthusiastically.

Before the two actually separated, Genesis kissed Samaria gently on the cheek as he leant towards her and bid her farewell, reluctant to depart but aware that time was not on their side. Although the lunch had been extremely enjoyable for them both, they both knew they had responsibilities in the form of work waiting for them as they rounded off their meeting. The two headed of in different directions as they went their separate ways and left each other's presence. Samaria rushed back towards work as she navigated her way through the hectic traffic of bustling passersby on the sidewalk, by now very much aware that her hour lunch break had totally been consumed and actually run out at least ten minutes beforehand.

Genesis regurgitated the contents of their lunch conversations as they continued to echo in his mind as he walked. The relationship between them he knew would indeed plunge him into the depths of foreign territory, in that he'd never actually dated a woman with a child before and he now he had to start to understand the deeper implications of actually doing so and the impact that would actually have. The intentions he had towards Samaria, had to be more serious and possibly more serious than they had ever been for any other woman he had ever met in the past. Whatever mistakes Genesis had actually made in his younger years whilst dating, the fooling around and engaging in relationships that were less than serious, with regards to Samaria, he simply couldn't afford to repeat. He couldn't put a foot wrong, he quickly concluded. The relationship he was about to offer her, had to be certain, he had to be certain and there was no room for any kind of disappointment on his part or any mistakes. He couldn't raise Samaria's hopes, a child's hopes and then shatter them, he had to be very sure.

The parking lot outside New Minds Inc. buzzed with activity as Genesis arrived back at work and glanced up at the building a little curiously. Everyone that he'd usually expect to find situated inside the building was now, for some strange reason standing outside and a puzzled expression crossed his face as he drew closer to the group of consultants. He quickly found Edgar and Raccoon as he searched the sea of faces that surrounded him for the two that were more familiar to him as he walked into the midst of the group of employees. Caton was nowhere to be seen.

"What's going on?" Genesis enquired as approached them both. "What on earth happened?"

"The building was evacuated." Edgar replied as he shrugged. "I'm not sure why."

"It's a procedural thing I'm sure. Disaster recovery, fire alarm drills and things, nothing to worry about." Raccoon replied.

His tone sounded reassuring but Genesis still had significant doubts as to the accuracy behind his words. Felicity and Caton exited the building a few seconds later as the consultants quickly gathered together in front of them.

Caton smiled as he attempted to calm everyone down and reassure them that the situation was under control and that there was nothing to worry about. "Don't worry everyone, you'll be back at your desks in no time." Caton reassured the group of anxious employees. "Just a practice drill in case of emergencies." His voice wavered slightly as his emotions betrayed him.

Lying wasn't something that came naturally to Caton and he was in unfamiliar territory as he attempted to lie to the faces of those around him, those he trusted and employed. The consultants that surrounded him waited for further clarity as to when they could actually return to the building and return to work quietly. Luckily since it was around lunchtime, none of the consultants actually had any clients with them when the building had been evacuated. However this was not going to be the case for the rest of the afternoon and Caton was well aware of that fact. The consultants would need to return to their consultation rooms, see clients and access the Adapt system.

A quiet, timid female consultant approached Caton called Mabel a little nervously as she sought to clarify what was actually going on. Caton had employed her a few years ago, when he'd found her working for a makeup line in a department store. He'd attended the store to purchase a present for a woman he was interested in pursuing and she'd attended to him politely. Mabel had then actually spent over an hour, fully identifying what would be the most acceptable and appropriate gift for his potential love interest and had gone out of her way as she'd studied the photo that Caton had provided to her, to accommodate his needs. The makeup she'd finally recommended had been accepted by the female appreciatively and he'd returned to the store impressed by her knowledge, to actually present her with a thank you gift. Unfortunately when he'd actually arrived on his second visit, he'd found

Mabel in tears at the side of the department store, devastated and distraught. The department store she actually worked for it transpired was actually being closed down and the staff had only just been briefed about its closure that very same day and Mabel was actually going to lose her job.

Like a true hero, Caton had ridden to her rescue and offered Mabel a job immediately. She had accepted his offer appreciatively, the salary he'd offered to pay her was a lot more than what she was used to and although she had initially doubted her abilities to actually perform the work he actually had in mind, she'd attempted to participate with a willing heart and grateful spirit.

"It's not that different from what you're doing now really. You give external makeovers to customers, just think of this as an internal makeover." Caton had explained. "I'll make sure the other coordinators give you a lot of training. You'll be fine. I promise."

The woman whom Caton had bought the actual gift for, Shelly had soon disappeared, due to his lack of attention and her lack of interest in him. Caton had been far too wrapped up and dedicated to his work around the time as New Minds Inc. had just opened, however Mabel had still remained. True to his word Caton had trained her faithfully and she had developed her skills over time, until she actually became one of his best consultants. She hadn't initially been as confident as some of the other consultants that worked for him, but she was just as competent and all the clients he'd assigned to her absolutely loved her. She had a way with people that other consultants simply didn't have and that stood her in good stead over the years as she'd built her client list and serviced her client's needs.

"Is everything ok Caton?" Mabel enquired politely as she spoke in a hushed tone and turned her back towards the other consultants nearby as she attempted to ask him the question she posed discreetly.

Caton felt slightly comforted as he smiled and nodded at her. "Everything will be fine." He insisted. "I promise."

The childlike qualities of innocence, trust and sincerity that encompassed Mabel's spirit was one of the things Caton appreciated about her. Whilst other people could be more calculated and at times even devious, Mabel simply wasn't. There just simply wasn't a devious or calculated bone in her body and her question had been posed with the deepest sincerity and concern.

"Everyone can go back inside now Caton." Felicity urged as she approached him and interrupted their conversation. "The system is back up and running and I've checked the security files. The breach is over."

"Right everyone back inside." Caton announced immediately, anxious to avoid any attention from any passersby and further potential delays to the rest of the day's work.

Whatever had actually gone wrong with the internal systems a whole company of employees stood in the parking lot outside the building was not a desirable image to present to the rest of the world and the whole incident absolutely irritated Caton as it scratched on his nerves. Felicity would find answers for him soon and things would return to normal once more. She absolutely had to.

RESTORATION OF INNNOCENCE

The rest of the week dripped slowly by as Genesis waited for Samaria to call and when the midpoint of the week actually arrived and he still hadn't heard from her, he began to consider the prospect that he might not actually do so. On the Wednesday evening he made his way home from work quite solemnly as he stopped off in the city to grab a bite to eat at a restaurant alone and a waiter showed him to a nearby table. The restaurant was relatively quiet and the food he ordered arrived ten minutes later as he began to wish that Samaria could actually be there beside him. He started to eat quietly and sip on a glass of red house wine as he attempted to satisfy his stomach which was simpler to satisfy than his present urge to see Samaria. He covered a mouthful of the steak he'd ordered with the rich, mushroom and cream sauce that adorned his plate as he glanced at his phone once more just to check and see Samaria had actually called or messaged him. His phone which lay silently on the table in front of him was blank and empty as it confirmed, she actually hadn't.

Halfway through his meal, the door off the restaurant opened as he glanced up and noticed Tiffany enter inside the restaurant. She noticed him immediately and made a beeline for him as she headed straight for his table. Genesis flinched slightly. Tiffany had been his first sexual conquest throughout the mind adaptation's experimentation he'd enjoyed, once he'd given himself a mind adjustment and the experience still lay fresh in his mind. He'd obviously not known when he'd met Tiffany, that at a later date he would actually bump into Samaria again and now he had absolutely no desire to rekindle the sexual intimacy they'd previously indulged in, due to his romantic interest in Samaria.

"Eating alone?" Tiffany ventured cheerfully. "Mind if I join you?"

Genesis had absolutely no desire to agree with her request but he knew it would appear rude and obnoxious to refuse to participate, especially when he was so clearly eating alone. "Have a seat." Genesis replied as he smiled at her. "I won't be here very long though I've got an early start in the morning." He continued as he quickly found an excuse to escape the possibility of lingering moments between them, that may lead to temptations later that the evening.

Tiffany smiled as she sat down next to him, comfortable and blissfully unaware of Genesis's change in circumstances and the arrival of Samaria in his life. The waiter returned to attend to her a few seconds later and she ordered some food quickly. He disappeared a minute later as he scurried off towards the kitchen to give them her order and the two continued to talk about light topics as Genesis continued to eat. Five minutes later the waiter returned with the food that Tiffany had ordered as he put a plate down in front of her and she smiled at him appreciatively. She tucked into the food hungrily as Genesis finished his own meal. He sat and watched her eat quietly.

ADAPTATIONS

A few conflicting thoughts crossed his mind for a moment as he contemplated further whether or not he should actually wait for her to finish eating before he got up and left the restaurant. He was a little unsure and decided to wait. It would be quite rude to actually leave whilst she was actually still eating. When the bill actually did come, Genesis fully intended to pay for both their meals it was the least he could do he quickly decided. He was aware that he hadn't actually wined and dined her at all the last time they'd met, when they'd actually spent a whole night together and settling the bill, he decided would perhaps ease his guilt a little.

Once Tiffany finished eating the waiter brought the bill politely as Genesis settled it as planned. The two left the restaurant together as they both made their way outside and headed towards the parking lot nearby. Genesis began to make small talk politely as they walked.

"It was such a surprise to see you here." Genesis remarked as he attempted to justify his lack of interest in her life.

"Well I don't usually eat here." Tiffany replied. "I just fancied a change and it was close to the hotel I'm staying at."

The two continued to discuss, laugh and joke as they touched upon the topic of the night they'd spent together as they walked. Genesis couldn't help himself as the two reminisced as he glanced at her body hungrily and digested the voluptuous, generous curves that poked out of the tight, short dress she wore. His sexual appetite began to growl inside him and lust for her as he yearned once more to actually be inside her. His body stirred as sexual arousal began to take over his senses and when they reached his car he was unable to resist the urge he felt inside him any longer as he pulled Tiffany towards him and slipped his hand straight up her dress. Luckily for them both, the parking lot was actually empty and relatively dark which allowed Genesis the freedom to express his sexual desires without any spectators as the darkness disguised his actions. Genesis touched Tiffany inside as he felt her wetness and she moaned softly in his ear, now he just simply had to penetrate her.

"I need to make love to you now." He whispered in a deep, husky tone as he felt the warmth and wetness inside her.

Tiffany giggled in response, put her finger on his lips and then grabbed his arm. She quickly led him back towards the street once more and then straight into the doorway of a nearby hotel as she smiled at him. Unable to resist Genesis complied fully as he completely forgot all about his intentions to make an abrupt departure from her presence as soon as their meal had ended. Now as he found himself suddenly lost in the lust and ravishing sexual hunger of the moment, he surrendered to the passion inside him that demanded immediate fulfillment.

Once inside the hotel room, the two made love vigorously and hungrily into the night as Genesis simply allowed his body to overtake his mind and control him. Tiffany complied with all his physical requests and allowed him to penetrate her in an animalistic manner as he ravished her body from every angle and position imaginable as she groaned and screamed with pleasure.

The next morning, when the two separated there were no explanations, no requests for further communication and no promises to meet. Tiffany asked for none and Genesis offered none. The crisp morning air hit his skin as he made his way towards his car, which was still parked in the restaurant parking lot nearby, sat inside his car and prepared to face the day ahead. His body felt slightly tired and although he could have headed straight to work, showered and changed there, Genesis quickly decided to actually rush home first instead. Turning up for work in the shirt and trousers, he'd worn the previous day wasn't a good look and Gemma the receptionist might definitely notice, he quickly concluded.

Once he arrived home, he showered, changed and ate breakfast quickly and then made his way towards New Minds Inc. as he considered his appointments that day and the tiredness he now felt. These all night sexual sessions just weren't practical anymore he thought as he stopped off and purchased a strong, black coffee on his way to work. He wasn't a young man in his twenties anymore. They were actually quite hard to keep up with. Twenty minutes later as Genesis arrived at work he made his way straight upstairs as he headed towards his consultation room and quietly contemplated what he'd actually done the night before. Although technically, he actually had no commitment as yet to Samaria, deep down inside his heart he couldn't help but feel as guilty as hell about what had transpired between Tiffany and himself the previous night. Inwardly the guilt gnawed away at his chest silently like a hungry rat and when Samaria actually called him later that morning, he felt even worse about it.

"I've managed to get a minder for Friday." Samaria confirmed enthusiastically as she greeted him. "And I don't need to actually collect Charlotte until Saturday lunchtime, so we can stay out very late."

From Samaria's comments Genesis could see straight away that she'd actually made an effort for him and he began to feel absolutely terrible. He'd already let Samaria down before their relationship had even actually begun.

"Great Friday it is then." Genesis replied as he accepted the arrangements and started to plan what they could actually do together that coming Friday evening. "We'll go somewhere really nice."

The call ended a few minutes later as Genesis began to contemplate what he personally had to do, to make sure that the relationship between Samaria and himself actually had a chance of survival. He was not the man he'd once been and in his current state, he knew he would definitely let Samaria down. Perhaps had to readapt himself and become the man he'd once been, the man he'd actually been for Cherise. Although there was no way that Samaria would ever actually discover what Genesis had done to himself or with Tiffany, the woman he'd actually spent the night with, inside himself Genesis wanted to be the most amazing partner she'd ever had and he knew in his present state, he simply never would be. It wouldn't be long before Genesis betrayed Samaria again, he thought as his sexual desires at the moment were too powerful and once they gripped his body, he simply couldn't control them. Genesis knew he had to make a choice for Samaria that involved a lot more than merely participating on and attending a date. He now had to actually decide whether or not to readapt his mind back to what it once was and whether he would actually commit to Samaria properly.

The day for Caton was productive as he met with Felicity and they discussed the attacks to the Adapt system together. Felicity smiled as she arrived inside Caton's office and sat down as Caton paced the room a little nervously. He glanced at her face as he searched for answers.

"I have actually got some answers for you Caton." Felicity explained as she glanced up at him. "It's definitely not one of your employees, you'll be glad to hear."

"Really? Who's actually responsible?" Caton asked. "I mean is it someone I know?"

"It's the female scientist you started the program with Alessandra, she's definitely involved." Felicity replied. "The man outside your employee's home apparently has aspirations to be extremely wealthy and unable to find a way to achieve this alone, he recruited Alessandra and they attempted to sabotage your operations, drain your systems of knowledge and even steal some of your clients. It's a sting operation, the two have attacked quite a few corporations over the years together. Apparently he supervised her first research post and that's how the two met."

Caton shook his head. "Why would she do that?" He asked curiously. "I mean I paid her well and I even offered her a job as I did with all of the four scientists I started the program with. They all declined as they had various other pieces of work they'd been commissioned to do once my project was complete and the Adapt system was up and running."

"Who knows Caton." Felicity replied. "People do strange things sometimes. I've spoken to your head of system security Raccoon and we've found a way to block them from accessing the system. So she shouldn't be able to disrupt the Adapt system any longer and you should be able to run your business in peace."

"What about the man?" Caton asked. "He was hanging around one of my employees homes."

"I've sent him a gentle warning and that should not happen again." Felicity insisted. "He knows, we know he's watching someone and he's been warned to stay away from all your employees in future."

Caton smiled as he rested against his desk and gazed into Felicity's eyes. "You're amazing Felicity. Really."

"Well I do try my best." Felicity replied as she stood up.

"Fancy lunch?" Caton asked politely. "My treat since you're all wrapped here, that means I have to actually find another excuse to keep seeing you."

"You know Caton you should really report this attack to the police." Felicity insisted as they two walked towards the door of Caton's office slowly. "If you don't they might try and do it again to someone else or perhaps even attack you again."

Caton paused by the door as he glanced into Felicity's eyes and then quickly looked away. "I can't Felicity. I just can't."

"Why not?" She urged. "What they are doing is criminal damage and theft."

"I just can't Felicity please understand. It would be totally impossible for me to do so." He insisted.

"Why Caton? Tell me why?" Felicity insisted as she demanded an answer from him.

"It's just well, it's just, well." Caton replied a little sheepishly. "Alessandra's actually my daughter."

Felicity shook her head in disbelief as she digested his remark. "Your daughter. How can that be? She doesn't have your surname.

You're not listed on any of Alessandra's legal documents as her parent or guardian."

"Her mother left me before she was even born. Another man." Caton explained as he glanced at Felicity's face a little awkwardly. "I was too caught up in work, neglected her and she left. She never came back and Alessandra came to find me herself when she reached adulthood. Of course I hired her to help me with the Adapt system in the hope that it would bring us closer together. Try to show her that I hadn't actually had a choice in her mother's departure and wanted to be in her life." He continued. "As you can see however she still clearly hates me and this is perhaps the one way of avenging and attacking what she feels robbed her of the father she should have had."

"I'm so sorry Caton. I had no idea." Felicity replied as she accepted the news. She paused for a moment before she continued. "You know I think lunch would be a great idea. I'm actually starving." She said as she smiled and touched Caton's hand reassuringly.

"Felicity we really should see each other a little more often. Seeing each other only when there's a crisis isn't a very pleasant way to retain, forge and sustain a decent friendship." Caton suggested.

"The ball is in your court Caton. I'm always just a phone call away." Felicity teased.

"Well I promise I'll make more of an effort to call you and see you." Caton insisted as he opened his office door and held it open for her.

"Promises, promises Caton. You're always so busy with your company, how would you find time for me?" Felicity remarked playfully as she walked out of the door in front of him.

Caton stepped out of his office behind her and then paused for a moment as they stood in the hallway and faced each other. "I'll make the time." He insisted with a very serious expression on his face. "I promise."

The two resumed their journey down the hallway towards the reception area as Felicity smiled at the thought of Caton actually making more time to see her. The idea of a lunch date excited her and the thought of a possible future romance with Caton wasn't something totally alien to her or something she hadn't actually wished for before, she'd thought about it a few times. He was a busy man though, just as she was a busy woman, but perhaps somehow in the midst of their busyness she thought, it might just be possible for them both to find some time and dedication to actually give to each other.

Life it seemed was definitely full of surprises and the closure of this investigation had yielded more results than Felicity could ever have imagined. Not only had she solved the case but she'd also solved the mystery of whether or not Caton actually had a romantic interest in her, something she'd often pondered about over the years, yet never had the courage to explore or attempt to determine, due to the professional nature of their relationship.

For once Felicity decided to succumb to frivolous desires as she wandered away from the usual, professional guard she kept up to protect herself from the possibility of any potential romantic disasters. Caton was a good man and just perhaps somewhere out there in the unknown future, there was a real possibility that they together might actually make a good couple.

The Thursday afternoon arrived as Genesis attended to his appointment with Titus and focused enthusiastically, motivated by Samaria's phone call earlier that day and their pending date. Titus arrived promptly as usual and had a big smile on his face, when he appeared. His presence and the nature of his appointments once more provoked Genesis's to consider that perhaps resigning himself to monogamy and faithfulness was actually subjecting himself to another miserable, unrealistic reality that would only ever actually be rewarded with pain. Genesis offered Titus a coffee as Titus sat down at his desk and faced him.

Titus accepted his offer appreciatively and then began to discuss his requirements for their session. "You know Genesis, I've met someone really quite special and I'd like to change some things." Titus explained. "I think I might even actually want to marry this woman one day."

Genesis who had by now sat back down opposite him and placed the two coffees in front of them both, almost spluttered as the mouthful of coffee he'd consumed on his return journey back to his desk, sought to depart from his mouth. He was completely surprised and stunned by Titus's request. Titus actually wanted to change. Titus actually wanted to become more faithful. Titus had actually even mentioned the 'M' word. He pinched his leg underneath his desk to make sure that he was actually really awake as he smiled at him.

"Are you totally sure?" Genesis ventured curiously, amazed at how one woman could trigger such a complete transformation in Titus's thinking.

"I'm very sure." Titus replied adamantly. "It was fun to have fun, but now I have to settle down. I'm getting older not younger you know. I need to have a family one day." He explained with a very serious expression on his face. "Orgies and families aren't really compatible." .

Genesis smiled at Titus's brutal honesty and sensible approach as he thought more deeply about himself for a moment. Titus was definitely right and in some small way he'd also managed to prod Genesis back in the right direction. Cheating, sexual promiscuity and families simply weren't compatible elements and Samaria came as a family package not a single ticket and Genesis knew it. Any doubts he'd had about reversing the process of his mind adaptations quickly fled from his mind as he humbly accepted Titus's wisdom. Samaria had actually been very honest about her responsibilities and her child and Genesis had appreciated that honesty, now however he knew he had to reciprocate that truthfulness towards her. He had to be true to her, be true to himself and be true to who he really was. He wasn't a cheat, a jack the lad and a player. He was Genesis, the type of man, a woman married and had children with. A father, a nurturer, a provider and a reliable husband.

"What if she leaves you one day?" Genesis enquired as he teased Titus a little curiously and played devil's advocate for a moment. "Will you regret changing, foregoing enjoyment and sacrificing all the experiences you could have enjoyed for her?" The question he posed although asked in a pragmatic fashion as if it only related to Titus's situation actually had deeper implications and Genesis knew it also related to his own situation.

"Relationships are always about sacrifice and commitment." Titus replied. "Sometimes the investment of your time, loyalty and dedication to the other person pays off and at other times it doesn't. We can't live our lives in fear of negative events that may never happen." He insisted. "Risk is not measurable when it comes to matters of the heart. If you lose and they hurt you, you perhaps learn a lesson, if you win and they love you, you enjoy everything you gain."

The logic Titus presented made total sense as Genesis agreed with him and touched the screen in front of him to access his profile. Genesis began to decisively push the negative doubts within his own mind firmly out of it as he accepted the truth in Titus's remark. He could actually reverse his own mind adaptations before he left work later that day and he too could try to be monogamous once again. Genesis simply couldn't risk bumping into someone like Tiffany again and succumbing to the desires of his flesh. Samaria didn't deserve to be dragged into that kind of mess, a mess that had clearly been caused by Cherise's betrayal. She was an innocent bystander that hadn't been involved in any capacity at all.

Cherise's betrayal had not only hurt Genesis at the time but now he quickly realized, he'd actually allowed her to control his life, his decisions and his relationships even after her departure. Even though Cherise had now actually moved on with her life, he hadn't, he'd allowed her actions to still influence his in a way that was immature, unconstructive and actually regressive. Instead of maturing gracefully, marrying and accepting the responsibility of committing to a life partner as he'd always believed he should, he now suddenly realized instead he'd actually reverted back to behavior that was commonplace amongst promiscuous teenagers that were unable to control their desires as they experienced raging hormones throughout puberty.

When Cherise had left him not only had she won the battle that he'd fought valiantly for her heart with his commitment, loyalty and devotion, she'd continued to win by damaging his relationships with other women also. Other women that might perhaps appreciate the gifts that he'd given her, more than she actually had. Other women who might actually want to spend their lives with someone like him. Titus was right Genesis couldn't live his life in fear that every woman he met might be another Cherise, another heartbreak and another let down. There had to be more to life and romance than just Cherise's disappointment.

Titus coughed as he lay down on the sofa nearby as if to remind Genesis off his presence. Genesis smiled and nodded at him as he quickly reassured him that he was actually attending to his needs and he hadn't been forgotten. He'd allowed his mind to drift off into his own thoughts and he had once again, almost forgotten that Titus was actually there. A strange thought suddenly struck Genesis as he touched the screen in front of him and Titus's mind map appeared, somehow as Genesis had fulfilled Titus's needs as a client, he realized he'd actually also been provided with some kind of healing therapy himself.

Up until that precise moment in time, Genesis hadn't actually realized how far from himself he'd actually drifted, until he'd actually seen his own reflection in Titus's situation. Samaria deserved more than a weak man with lustful sexual urges he couldn't control, Samaria deserved more than that from him. Samaria deserved what Cherise had been given but had never appreciated. Samaria deserved the real him. At that precise moment, Genesis made a very conscious decision as he grabbed responsibility and maturity by the arms and embraced them, for Samaria he'd return to truth, loyalty and sincerity, for Samaria he'd return to innocence, trust and respect. For Samaria, Genesis would actually return to himself.